FULL CRASH DIVE

ALLAN R. BOSWORTH

FULL CRASH DIVE

Allan R. Bosworth

COACHWHIP PUBLICATIONS

GREENVILLE, OHIO

The characters of the story are imaginary, and any resemblance to specific individuals, in name or trait, is coincidental.

Full Crash Dive, by Allan R. Bosworth
© 2017 Coachwhip Publications

Published 1942 from previous serialization
No claims made on public domain material.
Cover image: Submarine © MR1805

CoachwhipBooks.com

ISBN 1-61646-418-6
ISBN-13 978-1-61646-418-9

ABOUT THE AUTHOR

Captain Allan Rucker Bosworth (1901-1986), from San Angelo, TX, served in the U.S. Navy and U.S. Navy Reserve for 38 years. He honed his writing skills as a journalist and newspaper editor, going on to write numerous novels, short stories, and magazine articles, even during his active naval service. (*Full Crash Dive* was finalized "aboard a rolling and pitching destroyer in the North Atlantic patrol service.") He was especially prolific in Western tales. One newspaper bio notes Bosworth sold more than 500 short stories. He retired from the Navy to Roanoke, VA, in 1960, though certainly not from writing.

Bosworth's nonfiction included *New Country* (1962), the story of his mother and father as wagon-based wanderers, traveling from place to place until his mother (with ten children) finally put her foot down and refused to move any further west. His father shifted on, leaving the family behind. *The Lovely World of Richi-San* (1960) shared the story of Bosworth's time in Japan, as he met and befriended the Asano family in Tokyo, of whom only a young widowed daughter spoke English. She became Bosworth's guide and interpreter, introducing him to adventures around Japan, while exposing him to the tragic circumstances brought by war. This interest in Japanese people and culture, and a desire to expose an injustice, led him to write *America's Concentration Camps* (1967), an examination of the infamous camps where Japanese-Americans were interred (also discussing the highly-decorated 442nd Regimental Combat Team in Europe, made up of Japanese-American soldiers).

FULL CRASH DIVE

PRELUDE

Los Angeles, January 10—"Sit tight—we're coming!"

That terse message, flashed to the bottom of the storm-tossed Pacific early today by oscillator signals from the salvage tug *Algonquin*, spelled the difference between life and death for thirty-three men.

They were the captain and surviving crew members of the new submarine *Starfish*, which sank mysteriously off the California coast yesterday afternoon.

Twenty-two men are known to have lost their lives in the Navy's latest submarine disaster, and meager reports from the ill-fated undersea craft indicated that several others were injured.

Grim-lipped naval authorities, battling time and weather to rescue the survivors, refused to comment on the possibility that the new six-million-dollar warship may have been sabotaged. They pointed out that nothing definite regarding the sinking is likely to be known until the *Algonquin's* nine-ton rescue bell has brought its first load to the surface.

The *Starfish* was commanded by Lieut. Everett Brill II, and was the first of twenty similar ships to be constructed by Westco Iron Works. Two civilian employees of Westco—Victor Melhorne, chief engineer of the firm, and Foster Bedell, naval architect—are among those trapped in the ship they helped design and build.

Lieutenant Brill, member of an old Navy family, has seen his own career dogged by misfortune for several years. While executive officer of the destroyer *Bolton*, three years ago, he was court-martialed and cleared of charges of intoxication after the *Bolton* had rammed another ship in maneuvers. Brill's next post was command of a Yangtze river gunboat, which was beached and wrecked in a typhoon.

Brill is a "mustang" officer in Navy parlance, having come up from enlisted ranks after being dismissed from the Naval Academy because of a boyish prank. Officers who knew him said that he is a widower, and his 22-year-old daughter, Evelyn, is a nurse in the Navy hospital to which her father and other survivors of the *Starfish* probably will be taken . . .

1
FORTY FATHOMS DOWN

It happened with an incredible swiftness, and nobody could say how. After the first numbing shock had worn off and there was no longer anything to be done but wait and hope, Mike Way began remembering. He lay on a bunk in the crowded torpedo room and became conscious of ribs that pained him with every breath; he didn't want to think about those twenty-two men who couldn't get out of the after-compartments in time, nor to remember anything that had happened. But there was no helping himself.

It was like a jumbled nightmare, and the fragments of its horror were spilled across a man's memory in jigsaw puzzle fashion. The mind subconsciously groped for a piece at a time, holding it up to examine its fantastic shape and violent color, trying to fit it into a pattern of the whole. But this nightmare was not entirely over, and many pieces were still missing. . . .

Mike Way was a big man—so rugged as to be almost ugly—with twelve years in the Navy. He was a chief torpedoman, and a master diver. There was no responsibility for him, now—all of it had fallen on the shoulders of the skipper, yonder—and he could lie and taste the growing staleness of the air; he could watch the beams of the hand lanterns and flashlights that were used after the emergency circuit was cut off. He could study one taut, pale face after another, and feel the slow agonizing crawl of the hours.

He tried to pull his thoughts back to the present, and to project them into the future. It had not occurred to him that a man under these conditions was entitled to know a sweating fear. The haunted look in the eyes of that kid standing near the skipper—John Thorpe, his name was—came to Mike Way as a shock. The boy wasn't a day over seventeen.

Mike looked around him. Lieutenant James, the executive officer, a small and imperturbable man, sat on the deck forward. Lieutenant McQuaid—he was a junior grade, and the engineer officer—lay in the opposite bunk, seldom stirring, breathing loudly. He had managed to get out of the flooding after-compartments, with only two other men—and after coming through the galley door, he had desperately pulled it shut and dogged it down. . . .

That, Mike Way thought, took courage of a kind. It was a move necessary to save the ship and the men forward; it meant death for some of those who still were battling the slanting deck and the in-rushing water, aft.

McQuaid had dogged down the door, and heard two or three who reached it too late beating against the door with their fists. . . .

Mike Way's mind picked up one of those jigsaw pieces. It fitted in immediately after this scene. It was Cardoni, the dark-faced machinist's mate second class who sat yonder with grief and a sullen hate in his blood-shot eyes—Cardoni grabbing at McQuaid as he fought the door—Cardoni screaming that his brother was back there. And taking a swing at McQuaid while the slant of the deck turned so steep a man could scarcely keep his footing.

The two of them had fallen together, and other men came sprawling and sliding on top of them. McQuaid's skull was very likely fractured. Cardoni had broken his arm.

John Thorpe, the kid, asked in a scared voice: "Do—do you think it will be long, sir?"

"Not long, son," said Lieutenant Brill. "Stevens, try tapping again."

"Aye, aye, sir!" said the radioman. The electricity had been cut off to prevent an explosion caused by short-circuiting. To signal, now, Stevens had to swing a heavy sledge against the hull.

He tapped, and Mike Way studied Lieutenant Brill. He felt more sympathy for the skipper than for anybody else in this pigboat that lay forty fathoms down. And that went for the twenty-two men aft: they had died quickly, and Lieutenant Brill had died a thousand times, since. . . .

He was a stocky, graying man of forty-three who sat handy to the precious oxygen flasks. His cheeks were flushed, his eyes too bright. He coughed steadily. It would have been a hollow cough anywhere else, but there was pressure in the boat, and the pressure made all sounds flat.

Mike Way had done duty in the *Bolton* with Brill. And once, after a shifting sea had given him the "bends" in a dive, he had been a patient at the hospital where Evelyn Brill was stationed. He liked them both.

There was a chance, Mike Way thought, that this pigboat disaster would wash up the skipper's naval career and put him on the beach for life. He knew what the Navy meant to Brill. . . .

Thorpe said, "What time is it? How long have we been here?"

"Steady, son!" Brill drew his hand across his eyes. "It's half past three."

Eleven hours, Mike Way thought. They ought to be hearing the *Algonquin's* oscillator, soon—the electricity didn't have to be on to hear it if she was near enough. The eastern sky would be paling up there where the wind was sweet. Eleven hours since the skipper, keeping on schedule to the minute, had given the order for a full crash dive.

Mike remembered something else. Just before the dive. McQuaid, coming into the control room and asking the skipper if Brill was sure he was all right. Sniffing the air as he asked. Mike remembered how the skipper had stiffened and told McQuaid to get to his station.

Looking at Brill's flushed face, now, he wondered a little.

Another man relieved Stevens at the hull tapping. They stopped, awhile, to listen. And everybody heard the squeal of the tug's oscillator, all at once. Foster Bedell exclaimed, "Listen!"

"She's sighted our marker buoy!" Stevens said.

Men smiled. Brill opened the valve of an oxygen flask. New life poured into the thrice-breathed air.

"We ought to hear a diver on deck by daylight," Brill said.

Mike Way turned to ease the hurt in his ribs, and studied the two civilians—Bedell and Victor Melhorne. You expected courage on the part of Navy men; discipline had been hammered into them. It was gratifying to see civilians keep their nerve, too. Melhorne was stocky, with pale eyes and a tight mouth. Bedell would have been a few years younger, perhaps. He was obviously of a more high-strung type, slender and dark; he hadn't shaved for more than twenty-four hours, strain lined his face under its stubble, and he kept wiping his cheeks and chin nervously with the palm of his hand. But Mike Way had observed Bedell doing this before it happened; it was a habit, and if he was afraid now, nobody would have guessed it.

Lieutenant McQuaid turned as if in the restlessness of a delirium, lifting his bandaged head. He sank back, sighing, and mumbled through colorless lips. It was a meaningless babble at first, and then a few words became coherent:

". . . Brill . . . something. I know! I could smell it! Tell . . ."

The voice trailed into a babble and died. "Wop" Cardoni was straining forward, his eyes burning into McQuaid's face.

"I hope he dies!" Cardoni exclaimed. "I hope the so-and-so never wakes—"

"Cardoni!" snapped Mike Way. "Pipe down!"

"He killed my brother!" Cardoni said, and stared at the watertight door beyond which the tragedy lay. "He killed him just as sure as—"

"Break it up, there!" Brill called wearily. All the strength seemed to have gone out of the skipper's stocky frame. He coughed again, and his shoulders sagged; his eyes were still too bright, but there was a desperation in them, too.

"I could smell it!" muttered Lieutenant McQuaid.

Victor Melhorne met Mike Way's eyes. "He must be getting better," Melhorne said. "Think so, chief?"

Mike Way nodded. He had put that bandage on the gash in McQuaid's head, while Melhorne did his best to set and splint Cardoni's arm. There were several others suffering from cuts and bruises incurred when the *Starfish* slanted so steeply by the stern.

And the pharmacist's mate was one of the twenty-two, back yonder. . . .

"What time is it, now?" young Thorpe wanted to know.

Four o'clock. Thorne ought to be home, in high school, Mike Way told himself. A kid like that had no business in the pigboats; it wasn't right for a kid like that to know the horror Thorpe had gone through.

He was one of the three who had managed to get out of that engine room. McQuaid, Cardoni and Thorpe, running up a slanting deck with the black, rushing water closing over their frantic feet before they could make it—the water spilling over the storm step, threatening to fill the entire ship. . . .

Mike Way closed his eyes against the nightmare, but his mind would not stop picking up the fragments of its horror. The pieces didn't fit: there was nothing here to show what had happened to send the *Starfish* down so suddenly. She had dived before, keeping her trim and performing well. She had held close to the schedule Lieutenant Brill had laid out for her more than a week before the acceptance trials began. Mike remembered the morning orders on the bulletin board. "1530 Full Crash Dive. 1600 Surface and Proceed to Port."

It was 0400 now, by the Navy's twenty-four-hour clock. Dawn would be stealing over the sea. In Navy ships along the coast, the watch would be changing, and the ships' cooks were starting breakfast. In a little while reveille would sound, and the deck force would turn out to coffee and its job of washing down. The *Algonquin* was only a few miles away, and hope rode with her over the black, rolling swells.

There was nothing to do but wait. Rescue was paramount, now, and Mike Way knew the skipper was wise in speaking only of rescue, and not of the mystery of what had happened. They had reserve oxygen and water and food, and the skipper had seen to it that soda lime was spread in the torpedo room to absorb carbon dioxide. Time enough after they were out and up to consider the sinking. . . .

The hand lights were fewer and weaker. Mike Way's ribs stabbed him as he breathed the cold, thick air. He pulled a blanket around him, and grew drowsy.

A shout woke him, and he sat up in quick alarm. But the shout had been one of joy. Overhead, he heard the slow clump-clump of a diver's weighted shoes.

2
EIGHT WERE LUCKY

There was an eternity, after this. It passed for the most part in darkness; the skipper, between fits of coughing, ordered that the lights be carefully hoarded. Men huddled where they were, cramped and cold, because to move around or otherwise exert themselves meant to use more of the precious air supply.

Mike Way needed no light to see things just as they had been: Brill, sitting yonder, haggard and weary and feeling twenty odd years of Navy service caving out from under him—Cardoni's brooding eyes turned on the unconscious McQuaid—John Thorpe's frightened look, and the two civilians bearing up well under the strain.

Foster Bedell became talkative, now. It was a release from the anxiety that lined his stubbled face, Mike guessed.

"How many men can the bell take up at a time?" he wanted to know.

"Eight," Brill said, and coughed. "You two men will make the first trip."

Melhorne said, "That's not necessary, captain," and there was a quiet courage in his voice. "I think Bedell and I could wait."

"Sure!" Bedell declared. "I'm perfectly willing to stay until the last." His voice trailed off, then. "The more I think of it, the more incredible it seems! I wish I knew what happened."

Mike Way understood. It took time for the full force of it to hit a man. Melhorne and Bedell knew every rivet, every bolt in the ship. They had had confidence in her; in a large measure, everybody aboard had felt that confidence. It went with a new ship, proud and sleek and powerful. . . .

"Staying down won't solve what's behind that door, aft," Brill sighed. Another fit of coughing shook him. "That's going to wait until she's raised, I'm afraid. If they can raise her at all."

"Don't you think salvage can be accomplished, captain?" Bedell asked. "It surely wouldn't be more difficult than the raising of the S-4 and the S-51."

"Oh, it can be done," said the skipper. "I'm only afraid it will be delayed a long while. It's a long and tedious process at this depth and in these shifting currents. And the Navy may be needed elsewhere, in times like this."

The diver moved around on the *Starfish's* hull, groping for the escape hatch. Brill swung his flashlight beam to the overhead, and Stevens hammered the hatch cover with a wrench. They could hear the man outside working at the difficult task of securing the down-haul cable on which the huge bell would be operated. Mike Way began to feel fidgety for the first time; he knew every move that was necessary on the diver's part—he had felt the pressure that man was fighting at forty fathoms under a rolling sea. And he wished he could be in a diving suit now, helping. . . .

"I wonder if Lieutenant McQuaid will be able to tell us anything?" Melhorne asked, as if speaking to himself.

"That's rather hard to say," Brill said coldly.

Something had passed between those two, Mike Way decided. Something more than the incident in the control room, just before the full crash dive. Whatever it was, he told himself, it was no business of an enlisted man.

But he wondered if McQuaid would live to tell anything at all. His head had struck an angle-iron by the watertight door, and nobody needed to be a surgeon to see that the injury was bad. Besides, it was unlikely that McQuaid had had an opportunity to observe any more than Thorpe and Cardoni had seen.

These two had not been questioned, but in his earlier hysteria, Thorpe had cried: "The water! It came in—it came in from every-where, all at once!"

That, it seemed, was it. The water had suddenly rushed in.

The oscillator squealed, and men stirred restlessly and took a new, animated interest in conversation. The *Algonquin* said the downhaul cable had been secured, and the bell would soon be on its way down. There was a destroyer—the *Boone*—standing by, and others were earning to the scene. The *Boone* was waiting to rush the injured to port for hospitalization.

"Boy!" muttered a sailor in the dark, after this intelligence had been imparted. "Why didn't I bust a leg, or something!"

"They can leave me off at the dock," another said. "I don't need any castor oil or iodine—I need about six straight shots of liquor. Am I going to make a speed run when I hit the beach!"

It was rough, up there, the *Algonquin* added, and a new tenseness stifled the conversation almost as soon as it had begun.

"What if they can't make it?" Thorne's voice quavered. "I want out of here! I can't stand it. It's like—like a coffin!"

"Take it easy, kid!" somebody said gruffly. Nobody blamed him. The truth was, Mike Way thought, that everybody was really scared to death. An older man just knew how to tie down his fear and keep it in check.

Brill coughed, and said, "The injured will go first. That means Lieutenant McQuaid, Cardoni, Way—and who's that with a cut on his cheek?—Kowalski, Thorpe, Mr. Melhorne and Mr. Bedell. That's seven. Then in alphabetical order. You, Adams."

Adams, a salty first-class torpedoman, was holding a three-inch brass cartridge case. It was weighted with babbitt, and wired for a table lamp, with anchors and other decorations hammered into it. He growled, "Hell, captain, sir, I can wait," and hugged the lamp to him.

"You ought to go, captain," James said. The executive officer was calm, and assured. "Let me take over, sir. That cough—"

"It's my privilege to stay until the last," Brill said. He spoke simply, in a voice too tired to carry any note of heroics.

Mike Way raised on an elbow. "Captain," he pleaded, "you may not be hurt, but you're sick. Do what Lieutenant James says, sir!"

"That'll do, chief," the skipper called back, recognizing Way's voice. "You heard what I said. It's an order."

Adams chuckled dryly. "I'd hate to get a general court for mutiny on the bottom of the high seas. But, captain, you ought to go!"

It was a long while before the nine-ton rescue chamber came to a jarring rest on the hull of the *Starfish*. And it seemed even longer, after that, before the ballast tanks had been filled and the water was blown out of the bell's lower compartment. The men in the torpedo room grew restive, hearing the rescue bell crew working to secure the tie rods and open the hatch. . . .

Then quite suddenly, those below heard the hatch break its seal. There was a crack of light. It widened into a glow, and the air which flowed into the submarine was fresh and sweet by comparison. The hatch was open.

Men moved forward, not in any stampede toward escape, but impelled by the desire to look into the light—to see beyond the curbing steel that imprisoned them, and to breathe the compressed air that came from the surface.

"Hi, men!" yelled the dungareed sailor who peered down at them. "Who's going for the first ride?"

Lieutenant James exclaimed: "What happened to the captain? Bear a hand here, you men!"

Mike Way looked. Lieutenant Brill was slumped against the oxygen tank. And his chin was skinned.

"What the hell are you looking at me for, chief?" demanded Adams guiltily. "I guess the captain must have fallen over something in the dark!"

James grunted. "I guess he did, Adams," he said dryly. "Especially since he's sitting right where he was! Well, he goes up—he's a casualty, now. Bring McQuaid forward."

Mike Way swung his feet into the dirty water that covered the after portion of the deck. "Help me here, Cardoni," he said. "And you, Kowalski."

"I got a busted arm," Cardoni reminded him sullenly. "And I wouldn't help lift him out of hell!"

"Stow that sort of talk!" Lieutenant James warned sharply. "Give the chief a hand, there, Stevens."

They carried McQuaid forward, and hoisted him up the ladder. Mike Way couldn't lift much, because of his injured ribs. He turned his attention to the skipper.

When he put his good arm around Everett Brill's inert body, he felt something hard. A bottle. It was in the pocket of the skipper's dungaree jumper, and now that fresh air had diluted the mixture of smells in this compartment where men sweated despite the cold, he could distinguish the odor of alcohol.

Mike Way slipped the bottle from Brill's pocket without anyone's seeing, and dropped it behind the rack of torpedoes at his side. He was remembering that time in the *Bolton*, when Brill faced a court martial accused of being drunk aboard ship. . . .

They carried the skipper up the ladder. He was one of the first, and not the last, to leave the ship he had commanded and lost.

Mike Way was the eighth man. He was on the ladder when the chief yeoman handed him the log of the *Starfish*—a new book, and already closed.

"Better take this with the skipper," the yeoman said. Mike Way found a seat on the circular bench under the dome of the rescue bell. One of its two-man crew was down in the lower compartment; he closed the hatch cover on men who looked longingly on the light and still managed to smile.

"Shake it up, you guys!" somebody yelled from below. "Make your regular trip and return, cox'n!"

Then compressed air rumbled the water out of the ballast tanks and into the lower compartment. The rescue bell broke its seal on the *Starfish's* hull; it lurched, and started upward. The compressed air motor was put in reverse to act as a brake against the bell's buoyancy.

Lieutenant McQuaid, held propped on the seat between Foster Bedell and Victor Melhorne, muttered: ". . . smell it plain . . . I know that smell! My head . . . oh, don't, don't!"

They were nearly to the heaving surface when it happened. None of the rescued men knew exactly what had occurred, but there was a sickening, sidewise lurch as the swells took hold, and a thumping, rattling noise began under the wheel-locked hatch that covered the water-filled lower compartment where the downhaul cable was unwinding from its winch.

The sailor operating the compressed air engine yelled sharply, "Watch your heads!" and everybody lifted off the seat a few inches, and fell back, feeling the bell rocking slightly. It was like riding an express elevator until it strikes the safety cushion at the top of the shaft.

Mike Way realized they had stopped. They were on the surface.

"Jeez!" the engineer exclaimed. "Lucky—you eight guys are sure lucky! That downhaul cable's carried away. It's a good thing we didn't come up under the ship!"

Mike Way said, "Somebody will have to make that dive again!" and wished his ribs had not been hurt. The sailor nodded. The bell swayed as the hoisting cable attached to the *Algonquin's* boom took up the slack, and there was the welcome sound of feet on the topside of the rescue chamber.

The upper hatch opened.

Nobody in the bell had ever seen a sky half so blue, or tasted air so heavenly sweet as this. When a man climbed out, the wide horizons looked limitless after those crowding steel bulkheads. There was room here. Room to move in, room to live in.

3
THE ADMIRAL KEEPS A LOG

Admiral Wetherbee fidgeted in his bed in Sick Officer's Quarters at the naval hospital. This was like being in dry dock; it was no place for a man who had spent more than forty years at sea. He was getting damned tired of being cooped up.

The Admiral was an old man, and gaunt, but there were evidences that his age was mostly external—except for a brittleness of bones—just as a ship shows the years by a wearing of decks and companionways, and a mellowness of her woodwork. The Admiral's eyes were as blue as the sea that had been his life, and they could be as dark as storm clouds or as bright as sun-sparkled swells. He still had a voice meant to be lifted against a gale.

His eyes were dark, now, as he morosely regarded his starboard leg. It was bulkily encased in plaster, and hoisted, at an angle the Admiral estimated was just short of forty-five degrees, by a complicated arrangement of tackle and pulleys. No seaman, the Admiral swore, could have devised such gear. Irish pennants stuck out like sore thumbs in places where the line had been knotted. Not spliced, damn their lubberly ways, but *knotted!* The Admiral would have liked to give this modern, soda-fountain Navy a few lessons in marlinspike seamanship.

He wanted something to read. Particularly, he wanted the afternoon papers, which should contain something new about the rescue of the men in the *Starfish*. But he disliked appearing testy: the nurse or a hospital corpsman would bring him the papers, he thought, as soon as they had arrived.

He picked up Mahan's *Influence of Sea Power upon History*, and sighed because he knew it by heart and because he'd probably never go to sea again. He dropped Mahan on the deck by his bed, and followed it with the latest issue of *U. S. Naval Institute Proceedings*. There was a third book on his bedside table. He opened it and scanned its pages.

It was a Navy deck log, and fairly new, with only a score of its pages filled. The writing was a neat and precise script which neither hesitated nor grew bold. It was typical of the man. Nobody need be a chirographer to see that Admiral Wetherbee's penmanship denoted an alert and orderly mind, with a passion for detail and method where they were required.

The writing was small, like the ship models he made at home. Of all the ships the Admiral had sailed in, only his last—the flagship of the submarine force was not yet represented on his mantel. And the flagship itself had been half done when the Admiral slipped at the top of his cellar workshop steps. . . .

That mishap was duly recorded here, in the log, but Admiral Wetherbee would not have been guilty of referring to the cellar steps as such. The manner in which he adhered to nautical nomenclature may be gauged by a perusal of the full entry for that day:

> Anchored as before. 0915 Mustered crew on stations. No absentees. Made daily inspection of galley. LANI-GAN, Bridget, ship's cook, warned to keep supply of turkey legs in icebox. 1100 Made all preparations for getting under way via automobile for provisions. 1110 Got under way. Standard speed (30 knots) on course 170 True. At 1114, changed course to avoid heavy truck crossing bow. 1121 Moored port side of Main Street. 1150 Got under way for return to base. . . . 1314 Admiral J. K. WETHERBEE, U. S. N., Ret'd., (Commanding) suffered a fracture of the right leg when he fell down the after hatch. . . . 1430 Pursuant to the recommendation of Comdr. L. M. PHELPS (M. C.) U. S. N. Admiral Wetherbee was transferred to the naval hospital. . . .

The Admiral's shaggy brows pulled together in a fierce quarter-deck frown as he noted the date on that entry. More than twenty days. Bones knit slowly, at seventy. And twenty days in dry dock was a long time—especially to a man who never slept more than three or four hours at night.

It was time for those afternoon papers. The Admiral reached for his buzzer.

The nurse who answered was tall, and no costume would have been severe enough to conceal entirely the fact that she was pretty. He glared at her with mock severity.

"Yes, Admiral?" she said in a soft, well-controlled voice. There was no hint of strain in it, or in her face, but the Admiral knew she hadn't slept the night before. His glare was tempered by a light of pride—Evelyn Brill was Navy, clear through.

"What the devil are you doing on duty?" he demanded. "Didn't I tell you to get some rest? What good does your being on watch do?"

"I feel better, carrying on. This is my last day in S.O.Q., though—I'm assigned to surgery, starting tomorrow. Unsterile nurse, at first."

"Humph!" grunted the Admiral, and regarded her for a space. "Then I'll have to quarrel with somebody else. Unless I go to sea—oh, you needn't look at me like that! I may fool you. And don't twist those newspapers to pieces, Evelyn? Any news?"

"He's safe," said the daughter of Lieutenant Brill. "They brought him up on the bell's first trip."

Admiral Wetherbee's shaggy brows lifted slightly, but he tried to cover his thoughts. He said, "Well, thank God for that!" and smoothed out the papers. A big headline shouted: FIRST EIGHT RESCUED FROM SUB: SALVAGE CABLE BREAKS!

"That means," the girl said calmly enough, "that he's hurt."

"Not necessarily," the Admiral put in hastily. "There could be other reasons."

"To make him leave his ship? No. But I'm not afraid of the injuries. I have a feeling he may be blamed—officially—for the loss of the *Starfish*."

Admiral Wetherbee rustled the newspaper, and hid behind it. "Nonsense!" he growled. "Nothing to blame on him. I know submarines. They can be treacherous craft in more ways than one."

But he understood what the loss of his command could do to Everett Brill II. He had known Captain Everett Brill I, and he had dandled this girl on his knee when she was a baby. He could remember when he was commandant of the Academy, and young Everett Brill II was bilged out of the school. Twenty years, now, the Admiral had been interested in Brill's naval career. Telling himself that if a man were really Navy, he'd wind up with plenty gold on his sleeves, whether he wore an Academy ring or not. . . .

"The *Boone* is standing in," Evelyn said. "They'll be here, pretty soon."

The door opened. It was Dr. Vincent Ayres—he was a medical corps lieutenant—who respectfully awaited the Admiral's acknowledgment of his presence. He was young and blond with a long face that was both serious and sensitive and made him look older. He wore gold-rimmed glasses that somehow managed always to stay crystal clear, and his eyes were cool blue crystal beyond them. Eyes and glasses summed up the man's clear-headed, alert dependability.

He smiled at Evelyn. Just three nights before, they'd gone dancing. Off duty, it was "Evelyn" and "Vince"—and more than once in the past few weeks, she had had to remind herself that a Navy nurse had no business falling in love. You couldn't get married and stay in the Navy Nurse Corps. . . .

"Well, doctor?" Admiral Wetherbee grumbled. "I suppose you've come to tell me my request has been disapproved. I have a friend or two in the Bureau, and damn them—"

"No, sir," Vince Ayres said. "I don't believe it's been heard from. I came here after Miss Brill—I happen to have the duty tonight, and there's to be an emergency surgical case."

Evelyn looked up with quick intuition. "From the *Starfish?*"

He nodded. "We don't know who it is. Cranial injuries. Miss Welton's ashore. Could you—"

"I'll stand by, of course."

"Good girl! It'll be a few minutes, yet. I wouldn't worry."

He left to get ready for the operation. It was fortunate, Evelyn thought, that Vince Ayres had the watch; he was accounted the best surgeon on the station in cranial cases.

The Admiral knew this. "Good thing he's here!" he grunted. "Keep your chin up, young lady."

When the girl had gone, the old sea dog reached for his fountain pen and made an entry in his log. Long habit ruled him; wherever he might be, the log was written as though he were in command:

> . . . 1630 Word passed for surgery crew to lay to their station. BRILL, Evelyn, N. N. C., standing by despite anxiety. . . .

The ambulances had not arrived. There was a minute before the emergency. Before the surgery lights hammered a cruel glitter from scalpels and haemostats and retractors. Evelyn Brill leaned on the balcony railing, trying not to think.

She looked down over the drop of the rolling hills with their tall eucalyptus trees, down over the sun-bright stucco of the quiet town, and out to the blue Pacific. A wind was blowing, and she knew the sea ran high, but from this distance it looked soft and kind, with islands far out yonder like storm clouds melting into the water's rim. The silver sliver of a destroyer moved along the bay. The sun was low, but its red glint caught Navy wings high aloft, and a drone came to her ears as if riding that flash of light. She heard a radio playing softly in one of the wards.

She prayed silently. *Dear God, don't let it be Dad who is hurt! Don't let them blame him, this time. . . .*

And she remembered with a sudden shame that there were still men on the sea's bottom, out yonder.

She saw a heavy, important-looking man in civilian clothes pacing the sidewalk before the administration building, which was centered on the west side of the gardened quadrangle; he walked heavily, his leather heels slamming the concrete. Then the first ambulance growled into the driveway at the quadrangle's far end, and glided swiftly around toward the surgery building with a short, warning roll of its siren.

The other was close behind. Men wearing dungarees climbed out. One had his arm in a sling; another was limping. She saw a slender, dark-faced man in a gray suit—one of the two civilians who had been in the *Starfish*—and then white-clad hospital corpsmen came on the run to lift out a stretcher.

Panic seized the girl briefly. She couldn't bear to look on this—it might be her father. She turned her back on the green-lawned beauty of the quadrangle, on sunshine and fresh air. She went slowly into the hall of the surgery.

If Evelyn Brill had not been born a girl, Navy records would have contained the name of Ensign Everett Brill III, by now. Or, failing Annapolis as her father and many another good man had failed it, Seaman Everett Brill, working up from the ranks. She knew little of that civilian world the Navy pityingly calls the "Outside."

Her earliest remembering had been of gray ships standing in and standing out; of a jumbled, never-ending succession of greetings and goodbyes on Navy landings, where mist swirled and foghorns blatted and sailors wearing leggings and duty belts shouted a ship's name every time a boat bell clanged. Transfers—the tropics to Boston, San Pedro to Norfolk, Seattle to Pearl Harbor. Catch a transport. Sell the furniture. Drive to Philadelphia—and don't forget to change the oil in Kansas City. . . .

That was the Navy, and the Blue and Gold, so far as a woman was concerned. That was why, perhaps, Evelyn Brill was wary of falling in love with a Navy man.

A Navy doctor stood by when she was born. Everett Brill I—a commander, then—paced the deck of the hospital waiting room. His son paced the deck of a warship half a world away. And the commander assured Myra Brill that her husband's presence was entirely unnecessary.

"Hell, Myra," he told her bluffly, "just because a man's needed when a keel is laid is no sign he has to be on hand at the launching. I'll send him a radio the minute the boy's born."

There is only one way in which a girl who has betrayed several generations—by being born a girl—can join the Navy. That is to become a Navy nurse. Which is why Evelyn Brill was here, one of three hundred and twenty picked women, scattered from Portsmouth to the Philippines. Some of them were young and pretty, like Evelyn— but the Navy didn't tell them so. The Navy told them things like: "The waist, at the neck, must open not lower than two and a half inches from the interclavicular notch. . . . Sachet powder, perfume, or any unguent having noticeable odor is prohibited. . . ."

Evelyn Brill was loveliness wrapped in plain white drill. There was seldom anyone to exclaim over the discovery that her cool, impersonally efficient gray eyes could be strangely soft and warm; there were few opportunities for anybody to marvel at the shimmer of candlelight on the changing copper tints of her hair.

But over in S.O.Q. the old man whose sea-blue eyes seldom missed anything was indulging in one of his rare lapses when he permitted purely personal speculations to enter into his log. He frowned at the door for awhile, and then wrote:

> BRILL, Evelyn, deserves citation at meritorious mast. Romance? 1630, while word for surgery detail was being passed, sighted flashing light in eyes of Lieut. Vincent AYRES (M. C.) U. S. N. What's holding him back?

It might be stated that there were some who considered that the Admiral who kept a log had missed too many transports on the China station, which was the Navy way of intimating that his mind was not sound. But Vince Ayres, who was somewhat of a brain specialist and knew psychiatry, would have disputed this.

4
THE MAN WHO MIGHT KNOW

Vince Ayres shucked his uniform, and appeared in the hallway of the surgery in white cotton pajamas. He saw Evelyn opening the linen locker to get her cap and gown, and started her way, taking a last few drags on a cigarette.

A heavy, white-haired man puffed in from the stairway, perspiring and twisting a felt hat in strong, stubby hands. He halted, blinking in the dimness.

"Is this—will they be brought here? *Him*, I mean?"

Evelyn glanced at Vince Ayres. "One, I believe," she said. "The—the one with the skull injury."

"That's the one!" the man said. "McQuaid. The engineer officer. I've *got* to talk to him—I've got to find out what happened! I'm Martin West. I built that submarine!"

The elevator was whining up. Vince Ayres saw the girl close her eyes for a thankful space, and he moved quickly to her side. But she wasn't the fainting kind. He turned to Martin West, but before he could address the shipbuilder, a girl in a fur coat appeared from the balcony door. She was dark and attractive; Vince got the immediate impression that no expense had been spared in smart shops and beauty parlors to make her so. . . .

"Father!" she exclaimed. "You can't stay here. They've asked us to wait in the reception room at Sick Officers' Quarters. The men are being brought there."

West said, hoarsely: "I've got to find out!" But he went with the girl, and the elevator reached the floor, opening with a clatter. Vince

Ayres and Evelyn stood against the wall to let the stretcher pass into the anesthetizing room. Vince looked thoughtfully after the girl.

"Barbara West," he said. "I've seen her photo somewhere. Society section, I guess."

"That's quite likely, I suppose," Evelyn said, and the doctor turned to face her.

"Evelyn, I should have called on somebody else. But I thought you'd be under less strain, working. They'll probably put those men to bed at once, and allow nobody to see them, unless they got some rest on the destroyer. And—well, I wanted to work with you."

"I'm all right," Evelyn said, and managed a smile. "You'd better run along and get scrubbed up."

Doctor Brown, an older man and a lieutenant commander, hurried in to be Vince's assistant. A clatter of basins came from the surgery, where Miss Snyder had taken over as sterile nurse. And Mike Way came up the stairs.

He was in dungarees, his chief petty officer's cap set rakishly over a smudged forehead. Evelyn exclaimed, "Chief Way! I'm glad to see you again!"

The big diver grinned. "I'm glad to be here, Miss Brill. Your—the skipper sent me up to report. He—"

Evelyn drew a quick breath. "Is he badly hurt? Where is he?"

"They're turning us all in at S.O.Q. for tonight, and he's not hurt. He's got a bad cough, and looks to me like maybe he had some fever, though. Of course, the skipper is kind of dazed, and shocked. You know."

He gestured, and Evelyn knew. But there was something else she had to find out, as quickly as possible.

"Was it anybody's fault, Chief? Will they try to blame Dad, this time?"

The big man's eyes flicked away for a fraction of a second, then met hers honestly. "I don't think so, Miss Brill. It wasn't his fault—I'd swear to that. Somebody may try to lay it onto him, but if they do, it won't stick. You see, nobody knows, yet, exactly what happened. Unless it's the lieutenant in there—McQuaid."

He jerked his chin toward the anesthetizing room, and she thought his eyes hardened. She noticed he was holding one hand across his ribs after climbing the stairs.

"You're hurt!" she accused.

"Just a bruise," he grinned. "The ship went down mighty fast by the stern. Some loose gear carried away, and men were sliding all over the control room. I brought up against something, and there was a w hole pile of us at the galley door—the door leading aft to the engine room. Water started coming through there, and three men got out. McQuaid was one of them. He's the one who had the—nerve—to shut that door and dog it down." His grin was gone, and remembered horror twisted his mouth. Evelyn laid her hand on his arm.

"Don't talk about it, now," she begged. "You go and turn in. Tell Dad I'll see him after he catches up on some rest!"

The hospital corpsmen wheeled McQuaid past; it didn't take much ether to anesthetize a man who was already unconscious. Evelyn Brill went in the wake of the wheeled stretcher, remembering what Mike Way had said. Only McQuaid might know what had happened to send the *Starfish* so quickly to her doom.

She opened a swinging door, and the breath of the operating room struck her sharply, like a blow across the face with an ether-saturated sponge. Steam feathered from the bright chrome sterilizers and mushroomed against the drab leaded skylight. Incandescents beat down with inflexible brilliance; there were no shadows anywhere, and no coolness. Over all, the smells lay heavily: a miasma of carbolic acid, ether and iodine, steam-burned muslin, steam-baked rubber, alcohol's clean sharpness and tincture of green soap.

Hospital corpsmen were lifting McQuaid to the table. Under the anesthetic, his blue lips fluttered with each labored exhalation. The anesthetist lifted his ether cone and pinched the lobe of McQuaid's ear, watching how quickly the color returned.

"That pigboat must have hit something hard," he said. "Hard enough to throw a man down and fracture his skull!"

Another corpsman grunted. "It didn't happen that way. I talked to a couple of them guys. You see that one with a busted arm? They said he took a poke at this officer. The lieutenant dogged down that door, and this sailor's brother was behind it. I'd hate to be that pigboat sailor—you take a poke at any officer in this man's Navy, you're asking for a general court if he wants to make something of it!"

Evelyn moved a basin nearer the table, and busied herself with the sheet that covered McQuaid. Her cheeks were burning; there was a hint of trouble, here. Trouble for Everett Brill.

And the garrulous corpsman's next words were worse. He went on: "What's more, one of them guys told me that this lieutenant called the skipper down about drinking. There'll sure be a stink raised if this officer pulls through, all—"

"Hey, pipe down!" the anesthetist growled, with a quick glance toward Evelyn. Vince Ayres and Doctor Brown came in just then, and Miss Snyder, her apple-cheeked face half covered by the gauze mask, lifted a tray of instruments to the sterile table.

Vince Ayres' eyes smiled at Evelyn. "First case in surgery, eh, Miss Brill?" he asked, and chuckled. "The Admiral will miss you. Do you know what he meant when he spoke of that request?"

Evelyn shook her head. "No, but he's an old darling. I'll miss him, too."

"We all may," said Vince Ayres. "He's such a confirmed old sea dog he's requested—demanded would be a better word—transfer to the *Consolation*. He says if he's got to be laid up, he might as well be laid up on a hospital ship—at sea, where a man belongs!"

The doctor chuckled again, and then bent to his task. In an instant he seemed transformed into a stranger to Evelyn Brill—a cool, efficient stranger with marvelously skillful hands. And watching him, remembering the look in Mike Way's eyes and the thing the hospital corpsman had just said, she knew, for an instant, a guilty feeling: It was almost a wish that Lieutenant McQuaid would never recover consciousness. . . .

It was an hour before the doors swung open again. McQuaid, wrapped in white blankets, was wheeled toward S.O.Q. Vince Ayres peeled off his gloves and threw them on the sponge-littered deck. He went into the hall with Evelyn, breathing deeply of the purer air, and they saw Martin West pacing the corridor.

The other two civilians were with him, now. West, still perspiring, caught at Vince Ayres' arm.

"He'll live," Vince said.

"Thank God!" West cried. "You hear that, Victor? Thank God for one more saved! Oh, doctor—this is Mr. Melhorne, my chief engineer. And Mr. Bedell, the designer of our submarines."

"You were both aboard the *Starfish*, weren't you?" Vince Ayres asked in surprise. "You ought to be in bed!"

The stocky Melhorne's mouth tightened. "I couldn't sleep," he said, and his pale eyes seemed to see things beyond the white plaster wall. "Not—not while those boys are still down there!"

"They aren't out yet?" Evelyn asked.

"No—not yet," Melhorne answered. And Foster Bedell pushed his shoulders wearily away from the wall and wiped his cheek with his palm. The lines in his unshaven face seemed growing deeper.

"The divers are still having trouble," he said. "Heavy seas. But they'll all be saved. When could we talk to McQuaid, doctor?"

"I don't know that," Vince Ayres replied. "But not soon. He may not regain consciousness the minute the anesthetic wears off. There was pressure on the brain. It may take time."

Martin West turned jerkily. "Let's wait in the reception room, then. I want some more coffee."

Evelyn Brill got her uniform cape from the locker. It was blue, and lined with scarlet, and she didn't know how well it went with her coloring. Vince Ayres studied her while he got a cigarette and lighted it.

"It'd take more than coffee for me!" he said slowly. "I'd hate to feel responsible for having built that ship, in case a structural failure is found. . . . Evelyn, you must be fagged! You'd better turn in. Doctor's orders!"

She smiled faintly. The sun was down, and a chill had come in from the sea. She threw the cape around her shoulders, and shook her head.

"But I haven't seen Dad, yet, Vince. And, if I might, I'd like to stand by in Lieutenant McQuaid's quiet room. Please, Vince—there's a reason! I'd like to hear anything he says, conscious or not."

Vince's clear eyes studied her for a moment, then he patted her arm.

"I understand," he said. "I'll wait there with you. You run on over, and I'll be along just as soon as I shower and dress and make the rounds of the wards."

Darkness had fallen, but only a couple of table lamps burned in the big lounge that opened on the corridor of Sick Officers' Quarters. Evelyn Brill entered the dimness, and heard Mike Way say, "Here she is, sir!" And there was a stir, then, of men leaving to give her and Lieutenant Brill a moment alone.

She saw that rank had been forgotten temporarily, and that restrictions on visiting hours had been let down. The seven survivors who were able to walk had been billeted together here, and Martin West was going out the door with his daughter. Evelyn could look around the room and sense the loneliness that had filled it; the men had been sitting in a tight little group around coffee tables that were littered with cups and ash trays.

For the time being, she knew, all others—even Navy people—were outsiders. And it came to her quickly that there might be something significant in the fact that these men all had been kept together. The Navy wanted no false rumors to get out concerning sabotage, or anything else. . . .

Her father rose from a leather-upholstered davenport. He wore pajamas and a dressing gown, like the rest; she could see the strain in his face, and his eyes were too bright. Fever, as Mike Way had said.

They stood for a space, wordless. Brill's eyes were those of a man looking on something which is beautiful—something he had never expected to see again. Admiral Wetherbee's booming voice drifted down the corridor to break the silence. "But, damn it all, that's what hospital ships are for! And the sea's good for a man—"

A door closed, smothering the voice. Lieutenant Brill caught his daughter fiercely in his arms, but she could feel, in that close moment, that he was stunned and bewildered, with all the strength gone out of him. He held her at arm's length, and his palms were hot to her shoulders. She thought, *He's aged ten years!*

"Sit down, Dad." She wanted to cry, but the Navy doesn't do that. "You ought to be in bed. Mike Way is right. You're ill!"

He coughed. "I've got a little bronchitis. Nothing to worry about. Had it before we went out, but the schedule was all laid out, and—Evelyn, I ought to be out there now! Damn them, I belong with my ship! If I ever find the man who hit me in the dark, I'll have him court-martialed!"

"Sit down," she said, and pushed him to the davenport. "Nobody will blame you for coming up, Dad. And if a man hit you, it was because he loved you . . . the whole crew loved you."

"Loved me?" Brill's voice mocked the words. "Not all of them, Evelyn. Not McQuaid, in yonder. If McQuaid goes before the inquiry, he'll testify that I was drunk!"

"He couldn't!"

"Oh, yes, he could! I read rocks and shoals to him last week, and he's been nursing a grudge. Once in awhile, you find an Academy man who resents a mustang's being in command. Oh, they're very few, but there are some. McQuaid will make a good officer, in time. He just got his jaygee rank, and he's been a battleship sailor—he's been used to more military ways. You know as well as I that those things don't go on a pigboat, where you live so close to your men. You—"

"You hadn't been drinking," Evelyn said.

It wasn't a question, but a simple statement of faith. Brill recognized it as such.

"No, of course not. I wouldn't be so big a fool."

The others were coming back, driven by their lonely unrest. Evelyn patted her father's hand. "Don't worry," she whispered. "McQuaid will probably have forgotten the incident. It seems everybody's depending on him to tell them what happened."

"Maybe he can," Brill said. "Those other two men were in the galley, and McQuaid was the only one out of the engine room itself. Otherwise, we won't know until the ship's raised. All I can say is, it was quick and violent! Water must have come in by tons. . . ."

5
IN THE MIDWATCH

Mike Way approached the davenport, standing respectfully and looking down at his skipper. "Still too rough, sir!" he said savagely. "I wish I was out there—I wish I could dive!"

The little group sat down. A pharmacist's mate came from the hall, carrying an ice cap. McQuaid's ice cap. All eyes turned to him.

Martin West pulled himself from the edge of his chair. "Is he conscious? Can he talk?"

"He's delirious," the corpsman said. "Now and then he mumbles something about a smell. The ether, I guess."

West sank back, and the corpsman went into the diet kitchen. They heard him pounding ice for the ice cap. The blows echoed hollowly in the silence, and then Cardoni's bitter voice said, "I hope he never comes to! He could have let my brother out of there! He—"

"Pipe down!" snapped Mike Way. Everett Brill drew a deep breath, and went into a fit of coughing.

"I won't get over the tragedy of those men," West said shakily. "They've got to save the others—they've *got* to! I can't understand it. She was built right, I know. We've got six more like her on the ways, and thirteen to lay down, under the contract. If the *Starfish* had a structural weakness, I've got to know what it was!"

"Oh, the hell with what caused it!" Brill shouted. "There are still men down in that ship!"

"I'm sorry, captain," West said slowly. "I haven't forgotten them."

Evelyn looked down the long hall and saw Vince Ayres come in from the balcony, making his rounds. He stopped to consult Miss

39

Wilkins—she was the S.O.Q. night nurse—in her little office at the far end, and then he came to the reception room.

"This won't do, men," he said quietly. "You're all patients except Mr. West. Turn in, now. I promise to relay you any news as quickly as it comes. Mr. West, you and Miss West are at liberty to remain here, under the circumstances. But I'd advise a hotel."

"I'd rather stay," West said. Everett Brill rose heavily. "All right, men," he said. "Break it up." He kissed Evelyn's cheek, and Mike Way grinned at her as he passed, pushing his square jaw upward in a gesture that told her to keep her chin high. It also meant, she reflected, that he understood her father's worries.

Vince drew Evelyn aside. "I'll have to back down on that permission for you to sit out a watch or two over McQuaid," he said grimly. "You've got things to do. You're shoving off for sea at dawn!"

"For sea?" she echoed. "You're joking!"

"No, I'm not. The *Consolation* has been ordered to the scene, with some extra nurses and doctors and corpsmen. It's going to be a tough rescue job—we'll probably have a ward full of divers with the bends, and when those other men are brought up, they'll need immediate hospitalization."

Evelyn put hands to her temples to press out a thought. Just when her father needed her most . . .

"I'm going too," Vince Ayres smiled, squeezing her arm. "You'd better pack a bag, and get some sleep."

It was midnight before she had done with stowing crisp white uniforms into the bag at her room in nurses' quarters. Across the hall, Mae Kennedy was doing the same thing. Four nurses were going, Mae had said.

This was the Navy. Here today and gone tomorrow. As her father had been gone when Myra Brill needed him. Under any other circumstances, Evelyn would have welcomed sea duty. . . .

The telephone startled her. She thought, *Another emergency!* and then knew that Vince Ayres would have called on somebody else in that event. Perhaps it was good news, instead—perhaps Vince had word that the rest of the *Starfish's* crew had been rescued, and that the *Consolation's* orders had been revoked.

She lifted the receiver. It was Vince, all right, but his usually cool voice sounded tense.

"Evelyn? Don't be alarmed—your father is quite all right. It's Mc-Quaid."

Evelyn caught her breath. "He's dead!" she said with a sudden prescience. "Vince—he's dead!"

"Come over to S.O.Q. at once," Vince Ayres said. "He didn't just—just die, Evelyn. He was murdered—clubbed to death in his bed."

She never remembered leaving the nurses' quarters. She found herself stumbling along the hedge-rimmed walk, with a fine, blowing drizzle cool against her cheeks in the dark. Somebody moved yonder with a flashlight, and she heard men calling to one another. An automobile swung around the driveway to catch her full in the glare of its lights, startling her. It sped to the curb before the administration building and stopped there with a squeal of brakes.

She saw Captain Jessup jump out. He was the medical corps four-striper commanding the hospital, a little, bald man of about sixty. He slammed the car door and hurried inside, and Evelyn heard loud voices in the personnel office where the chief pharmacist's mate of the watch and the master-at-arms force had their headquarters.

She took the stairs, and arrived breathless in the entrance of the reception room at S.O.Q. All the lights were on, now, and there was a semi-circle of white, drawn faces; at first glance, it appeared that everybody who had been in the room earlier was again on hand, sitting and facing Vince Ayres. She saw her father, looking more stunned than before. Mike Way's rugged features were set in bleak, hard lines.

Vince came toward her, gravely. She heard Cardoni's voice, no longer bitter. "I didn't mean what I said! I didn't mean what I said about wishing he'd die!"

Vince took her arm. "Evelyn," he said so low the others couldn't hear, "I hate to drag you into this . . . but they'd have called you, anyway. And you can help. Keep your eyes and ears open, and watch everybody! There's one man missing. The youngster—Thorpe."

"That kid? Vince, he couldn't—"

"Here comes the captain," Vince interrupted.

Jessup was more the physician and surgeon than an administrative officer. He tried, now, to keep the anxiety out of his voice, and to sound military.

"What steps have you taken, Dr. Ayres?"

"The master-at-arms force and the civilian night watchman are watching the fence, sir," Vince reported. "I notified the marine sentry at the gate to allow no one to leave the grounds, and I called out the marine guard to search them. Nobody's gone out the gate in the last two hours, except Mr. West and his daughter. They grew tired of waiting here, and left for their hotel. That was forty minutes ago, according to the gate sentry. I've telephoned for them to return."

"You didn't notify civil authorities—the police?"

"No, sir."

"Good. I'll report to the Commandant as soon as I learn the details. If police were called in, the newspapers would be on our necks and linking this—er—affair to the *Starfish* disaster. We must try to keep down the scandal. Now, suppose you tell me everything you know."

"Yes, sir." Vince drew a deep breath; his long, sensitive face was pale and solemn, but his eyes behind their glasses appeared as cool and clear as ever. Evelyn found a seat beside her father. Everett Brill took her hand and held it tightly. His palm was sweating, now; the fever, she thought with relief, was broken. She saw that the night nurse, Miss Wilkins, had joined the group, and there were two corpsmen—both looking frightened.

"McQuaid was in Number Five quiet room, sir," Vince Ayres began. "Number Three is unoccupied. Admiral Wetherbee is in Number One, and Lieutenant Brill was in Number Seven. All the odd numbers have windows opening on the balcony."

"I know that," Captain Jessup said impatiently.

A buzzer sounded in the hall. Miss Wilkins said, "That's the Admiral. Answer it, Murphy."

"He was killed just before midnight, sir," Vince went on. "The corpsmen were changing watches. Miss Wilkins was in the diet kitchen, getting"—a trace of ironic amusement touched his voice—"a cold turkey leg for the Admiral. Murphy was relieving Jacobs as the special watch over McQuaid. They both went into the diet kitchen, too—Murphy to refill McQuaid's ice cap, and Jacobs to get Lieutenant Brill something to eat."

The captain glanced at Brill. "At midnight?"

"Yes, sir," said Brill, flushing. "I couldn't sleep. I hadn't eaten for twenty hours. I called him as the watch was changing, and asked for a couple of three-minute eggs."

"When Murphy went back to Number Five," Vince resumed, "he found McQuaid dead. Or, rather, dying. He was still breathing, then."

"Who's Murphy?" the Captain asked.

"The redheaded corpsman, Captain," Miss Wilkins said. "He's answering the Admiral's bell. Here he comes, now."

"Doesn't the Admiral ever sleep?" demanded Jessup. "What did he want now—another turkey leg?"

"No, sir," Murphy answered. "He wanted his fountain pen filled. He's writing in his log, sir—an entry about the murder, he said."

Vince Ayres looked queerly at Evelyn. Captain Jessup cleared his throat. "Murphy, how long were you out of the quiet room?"

"About five minutes, sir. I had to chop some ice—and then—"

He hesitated, and Captain Jessup turned on Vince Ayres again. "Go on, doctor. Did you find the murder weapon?"

"Not yet, sir. We found the window open. But I looked for wet footprints in the room, and there were none. Then"—he reached into the seat of a club chair—"we found this. On the balcony."

He held it up. Evelyn saw it was a scarlet-lined nurse's cape. *Her* cape! There was a darker stain against the crimson lining, and the rain had already started. spreading it. . . .

Vince Ayres' voice sounded flat, deadly: "Apparently it was used to wrap the murder weapon, Captain. The weapon would have been heavy, and blunt; this cape not only averted the chance of fingerprints, but deadened the sound of the blows. McQuaid's skull is badly crushed. Perhaps you'd like to look at him—"

"Not yet!" said Jessup. He took the cape, and looked up sharply. "Yours, Miss Wilkins?"

She was a mouse-like woman of past forty. She gasped, "Heavens, no, Captain!"

"It's mine, Captain Jessup," said Evelyn Brill calmly.

She felt her father's hand tighten spasmodically. Mike Way's eyes were on her, and those of all the others: she could feel them. Only Vince tried to look elsewhere, and she remembered what he had said . . . *they'd have called you, anyway.* . . . Out of the corner of her eyes, she could see Victor Melhorne's heavy face; there was almost accusation in his pale, unwinking stare. Foster Bedell rubbed a palm across his stubbled cheek, and the beard made a rasping sound. . . .

"Do you know how it got there?" Captain Jessup was asking her.

"No, sir. I—I think I must have left it here, in this room." She felt confused; after the shock of the telephone call, she hadn't remembered going into the rain without a cape. But her white uniform was damp.

"Miss Brill left here hurriedly, to pack and get some rest," Vince was explaining, kindly. "She's one of the draft for the *Consolation*, Captain. And she's been under a considerable strain. I—"

Someone was coming up the stairs. Everybody looked that way, and saw Martin West puffing into view. Barbara West was holding his arm. She had removed a portion of her makeup at the hotel, and had had no time to renew it. Her heavily mascaraed lashes were incongruous against her pale cheeks.

"My God!" West panted. "The one man! The one man who knew! Who did it, doctor—who killed him?"

"Sit down, Mr. West," said Vince. He pulled out the club chair for Barbara. "That's what we're trying to find out, and you may be able to help us."

West raised his stubby hand quickly. "I don't know anything about it—not a thing! And neither does my daughter."

"None of us does," Vince said patiently. "But you and Miss West had an advantage. You left at the approximate time the murder took place, and you were out here, where you could see anyone who came in or went out—something none of the others could notice from their rooms. Did you see anybody?"

"Not a soul!" West said emphatically. "Not a—"

"Father," the girl said. "There was one man. Remember—the young sailor? Thorpe, his name is, I believe. He came through here and went out on the balcony, before we left."

"That's right," nodded West. "I'd forgotten."

Vince Ayres' face was a grave mask. "How was he dressed?"

"Why—he was wearing pajamas and a robe. Like all the others," Barbara West said. "I remember his eyes. He looked—well, dazed, and frightened."

Mike Way snorted. "The kid has been scared to death since it happened, doctor. Surely nobody thinks he killed the Lieutenant!"

Vince turned to Everett Brill. "I'm not thinking he did," he said. "But he's the only one missing, and we've got to check up. Lieutenant Brill, in your opinion would Thorpe have had any reason to commit such a crime—taking into consideration his mentally disturbed state, which might have magnified a small resentment out of all proportion? Was there a grudge that you know of?"

"McQuaid," Brill said slowly, "put the boy on report—twice. But, good God—that's nothing! That's no grounds for suspecting Thorpe! He's just a kid. Why—"

The Admiral's buzzer sounded again. Murphy arose with a resigned air, and went down the hall. Captain Jessup fidgeted. "I suppose I'd better notify the Commandant," he said. "Dr. Ayres, you carry on. Nobody is to leave this room. If Thorpe is found, I want to be notified at once."

"Aye, aye, sir!" Vince said.

Murphy came back, carrying a book. "It's the Admiral's log, sir," he reported as he handed it to Vince Ayres. "He says he hasn't been asleep yet, tonight, and he's jotted down his observations here. Wants you to read it."

Vince Ayres turned the pages half-curiously, half-humorously, until he reached the last entry. He studied this a minute in silence, then looked up.

"Insomniacs," he said slowly, "are usually cursed with over-active imaginations. But Admiral Wetherbee has well-developed powers of observation, as well. I'm going to read what he's logged, tonight. If anybody chooses to take offense—I'll ask you to remember that this is a murder, and that none of us is entirely free of suspicion until the murderer has been found."

He lifted the logbook, and began reading:

10 January (*Continued*)

In dry dock, as before.

1640 First rescued survivors of *Starfish* reported aboard, several suffering from injuries.

1700 Lieut. (jg) Frederick McQUAID, U. S. N., underwent operation for fracture of skull.

1930 Admiral J. K. WETHERBEE notified request for transfer to hospital ship *Consolation* approved.

1930 to 2300 Preparing to get under way for sea.

2400 Lieut. (jg) Frederick McQUAID found murdered in Room Five, this station. Who . . . and why? Mysterious incidents noticed, remarks overheard, etc., include:

At about 2000 man identified as CARDONI, John Joseph, M. M. 2c, U. S. N., of *Starfish* survivors, heard to express hope McQuaid would die. At about 2310 a woman's figure hesitated on balcony outside my window. Appeared to be wearing nurse's cape. But nurses' shoes have flat, rubber heels, do not click. Nurses not allowed to wear perfume. . . .

Barbara West gasped. "That is a deliberate attempt to insult me, doctor!" she exclaimed angrily. "It's obvious that I am the only such woman at this hospital tonight. I won't listen to that sort of nonsense! Father, please take me back to the hotel!"

Martin West half rose, but Vince Ayres motioned for him to remain seated.

"I must remind you again," he said gently. "The gate is guarded. Nobody can leave. Now, if you'll permit me to finish reading . . ."

At approximately 2330 a man's figure passed open window in rain. He was carrying something over his shoulder. It might have been a swab handle, or something heavier.

Motives for murder: Revenge? Possible, but not likely. Jealousy? Must inquire into any love affairs McQuaid had. Most likely motive hinges on fact McQuaid was apparently only man who knew what happened in *Starfish's* after-compartments to sink ship. McQuaid heard, while delirious, muttering about smell. What sort of smell? Ether . . . whiskey . . . something in submarine . . . What? Must find out.

Vince Ayres put down the book, and then, as an afterthought, handed it to Murphy.

"Return it to the Admiral with my thanks," he told the corpsman. "Tell him I'll talk to him later about the case, and congratulate him for me on the fact that he's going to sea, after all."

There was a commotion at the stairway entry. A member of the master-at-arms force appeared with the old civilian night watchman. They were dragging a man between them—a slender figure in a rain-sodden bathrobe.

"Thorpe!" exclaimed Lieutenant Brill.

Vince Ayres nodded impassively, and the two brought Thorpe forward and pushed him into a chair. He had a fresh scalp wound high on his forehead, and he looked to be only half conscious. He was sobbing in convulsive jerks.

"Get some aromatic spirits, Miss Wilkins!" Vince said. "Where'd you find him, McCarthy?"

"Walking by the west fence," said the watchman. "Carrying this."

He handed Vince a broken billiard cue. It was wet by the rain.

Foster Bedell shuddered. "My God!" he murmured. "He couldn't have done it! Why—he just isn't the kind! Where'd he get that cue?"

"There's an old table in the corner, yonder," Vince said slowly. "McCarthy . . . did he offer resistance? Is that where you hit him?"

The night watchman nodded. "Yes, sir. I had to. He came walking straight at me, and he was carrying that shillaly like a gun. I hollered for him to halt and put it down, but he came on. I dodged, and tapped him with my billy."

Miss Wilkins forced the aromatic spirits into young Thorpe's mouth. He coughed, and sat up more erectly. His eyes lost their dazed expression.

"All right, Thorpe," Vince said. "Talk up. What were you doing out in the compound? What were you doing carrying this club?"

"I—I don't know!" the boy said. "I don't remember. . . . I went to bed, and . . . I don't know!"

"Try to remember—try hard," Vince said grimly. "Something has happened, and you may find yourself in a bad spot unless you can explain. Where'd you get this billiard cue?"

Thorpe shook his head. "I didn't know I had it, sir," he said dazedly, and passed his hand across his brow. "My head—it's bleeding! What happened?"

"Take it easy, Thorpe," Vince cautioned. He examined the cut. "This will need a couple of sutures. Miss Wilkins, if you'll get me a surgical kit—"

The abrupt, excited entrance of Captain Jessup interrupted. The hospital commander faced Martin West's chair angrily.

"Mr. West, did you tell the newspapers about this?" he demanded.

"Why, no, certainly not!" West said. "I—I told them that I planned to take my own salvage equipment to sea, if the Navy will let me. The reporters left. I'm afraid I did mention the murder to the hotel clerk as we left, though. I—I was very upset."

Jessup boiled over. "That was very thoughtful of you, sir! Now there are a dozen reporters and cameramen at the gate!"

"I'm sorry, Captain," West said contritely. He looked helpless at the moment for all of his stocky, aggressive build.

"I've some news for all of you—Mr. West included," Jessup snapped. "The Commandant has instructed me to order you all aboard the *Consolation* at dawn!"

A murmur rose. It came from West and his daughter, and from Victor Melhorne and Foster Bedell. Navy people, being that, said nothing.

"But I can't go!" West protested. "If I could help, of course, but— And I need Melhorne and Bedell at the yards!"

Captain Jessup eyed the civilian group with something like disdain. Barbara West's pale face clearly showed the distaste she felt; a luxury liner, Evelyn thought, would be more according to the girl's choice. . . .

"Everybody who was in S.O.Q. is to be kept together," Jessup said. "The inquiry into McQuaid's murder will proceed aboard the

Consolation. Dr. Ayres, I'll give you written orders placing you in charge for the present. There'll be no newspapermen out there—not on the *Consolation*, at least."

Vince said, "Aye, aye, sir!" and looked at Evelyn Brill. Neither had ever dreamed of going to sea under such circumstances.

6
SAIL BEFORE SUNUP

Vince Ayres felt more like a cop than a Navy medical officer. He stepped out of the first station wagon as it halted on the dock, turning up his raincoat collar and watching two other machines come to a stop. Wind whipped the drizzle into a soft mist that was like a thin, wet curtain fluttering against your face. Lights dripped and ran in reflected pools; the dock's asphalt and worn timbers might have been mahogany. The gangplank creaked to the rise and fall of the ship, and black water sucked noisily under the pier pilings.

He turned his back to the wet wind, and checked the muster list of the party as they went aboard the *Consolation*. Admiral Wetherbee's stretcher went first, manned by a pair of hospital corpsmen; they carried him properly up the gangway, head first, but he let out a sea dog's bark as they reached the deck.

"Way enough!" the Admiral boomed, and sat up rigidly to face in the direction of the quarterdeck and saluted. "Carry on," he said, when this respect had been paid. Watching, Vince wished the *Consolation* had been notified that the Admiral was coming. It would have been nice, he thought, to see side-boys pipe the old man aboard in style.

He checked the names. Nurses were next. Mae Kennedy, Miss Malone, Miss Ballew, Evelyn Brill, and the drab little Miss Wilkins, who'd been on duty in S.O.Q. Lieutenant Brill was holding his daughter's arm; a borrowed raincoat covered his stocky form.

Vince touched Evelyn's arm. "See that he has some cough medicine before he turns in," he said, and she smiled gratefully.

51

There was strain on all these faces, and a bewilderment no one could leave ashore. Victor Melhorne and Foster Bedell waited at the gangway for Martin West and his daughter to precede them. Odd thing, Vince thought—civilians boarding a Navy ship, going to sea . . .

Barbara West lifted her expensive fur coat and the gown that was beneath it as she crossed the wet gangplank. Navy men followed. Even in civilian clothes, Vince thought, he would have known they were Navy men: it was in their manner of going aboard, and the way they saluted both the gangway and the officer of the deck. Young John Thorpe, his eyes wide and haunted under the strip of adhesive that covered the scalp cut—halting briefly, looking down at the dark, noisy water—and Cardoni, his dark face grown more stolid. Kowalski, a square-faced man with his curly head bare, and one cheek bandaged. Then Mike Way.

The big chief torpedoman alone seemed alert. Fatigue dropped easily from his rugged frame, and his bruised ribs had been taped so that he no longer had to hold his hand against the pain of his breathing. He stopped, and saluted.

"Doctor Ayres, sir, I want to put in a request. I want to be sent over to the *Algonquin*, so I can dive."

Vince smiled. "Take it easy, chief! Haven't you had enough trouble? You wouldn't want to come up with bends!"

"No, sir. But I could stand the pressure. I could get that cable secured to the *Starfish*, sir! Will you let me dive?"

"We'll see, later," Vince said. He patted the big man's arm. "Get some sleep, now."

"Aye, aye, sir."

Vince Ayres understood. Twenty-five men still down there in the submarine. Shipmates of Mike Way, as those who had died had been shipmates. The word means something, in the Navy. . . .

He checked off the hospital corpsmen who had been sent along. They included the two men who had been in Sick Officers' Quarters when McQuaid was murdered—Murphy and Jacobs. Then he went aboard, and a deck detail at once began shipping the gangplank. The *Consolation* was sailing before sunrise.

She had just been commissioned in the Navy, but she was old in sea service. Formerly a passenger vessel of some nine thousand tons, she had been replaced in the coastal run by larger and more luxurious liners after war abroad shut down on transatlantic sailings. The Navy bought her, knocked out some of the cabin bulkheads to create wards on both the main deck and the promenade deck, and installed hospital equipment—including a well-lighted operating room aft over the fantails.

The *Consolation* gleamed palely in the wet dawn, under her fresh coat of white paint. She looked like a ghost ship—and she was so empty of personnel, Vince found, as to further this illusion. Only a skeleton staff of the doctors, nurses and corpsmen she would need had so far been put aboard. The deck force was billeted in the focsle, and this left more than a score of rooms that had once been passenger cabins available for the party that had just come aboard.

Assignment of quarters found the enlisted men chortling that at last they had found a Navy they liked. They were paired in the rooms that had once been tourist class cabins. The nurses and Barbara West had rooms to themselves, as did Vince Ayres and Everett Brill. Admiral Wetherbee was already being made comfortable in a roomy cabin aft; Martin West, Foster Bedell and Victor Melhorne were established amidships.

"Everybody," Vince told them, "will muster in that small isolation ward on the main deck at eleven o'clock, so we can resume the investigation. You'd better sleep fast!"

He turned in. Yesterday seemed an age ago—an eternity crowded with incredible things. The full horror of McQuaid's murder struck him as he lay wide-eyed, feeling the tremor of the engines and the beam roll that began when the *Consolation* backed into the bay. A weariness lay heavily upon his eyelids, but his thoughts ran restlessly while light grayed in the porthole glass. He thought of Everett Brill— the submarine skipper had taken a room two decks down, where he would feel more at home. He thought of the others, considering one by one the persons who had been in S.O.Q. before and after somebody—*one of them*—slugged an unconscious man to death. But there was no really tangible clue remembered; there was nothing on which his fatigue-fogged mind could base the foundation and rear the structure of the crime.

He came, then, to more pleasant thoughts. Evelyn Brill. With changing ballroom lights on her coppery hair, and the whisper of her evening gown in his arms. She had still been beautiful under those other lights—in the harsh brilliance of the surgery. Still beautiful, but very impersonal, and far away. It was hard to disassociate her from the Navy . . . and those few women who were in the Navy couldn't get married. . . .

In a room on the starboard side of the main deck, Admiral Wetherbee shook ink into the point of his fountain pen. It was no trick at all for a man accustomed to only three or four hours sleep nightly to do without sleep entirely. He propped his back against the pillows and made an entry in his logbook.

> U. S. S. *Consolation* 11 January.
> Moored as before.
>> 0500 Made all preparations for getting under way.
>> 0505 Pursuant to orders of Commandant, Admiral J. K. WETHERBEE, U. S. N. (Retired) reported on board with hospital draft in command of Lieut. Vincent AYRES, (M. C.) U. S. N.
>> Murder inquiry ordered to convene at 1100.
>> 0530 Dispatched urgent message to Commandant to advise course of procedure in regard to Lieut. Everett BRILL, U. S. N., captain of the late U. S. S. STARFISH.
>> 0600 Got under way for scene of STARFISH disaster. Captain at conn, Navigator on the bridge, standard speed, standing out of harbor on various courses conforming to the channel.
>> NOTE: Why did no one in S.O.Q. hear blows of weapon used in murder of Lieut. McQUAID? Blows of force sufficient to crush man's skull are not exactly silent, and several men were within earshot. Must consider this important question.

Vince Ayres entered the isolation ward at two minutes before eleven, and rapidly ran his eye over the group assembled there. He said, "Good morning," and the chorus of greeting reminded him of school days. Everybody, he noticed, appeared freshened.

"Chief," he told Mike Way, "I'll appoint you master-at-arms. Your first job will be to see that Murphy and Jacobs muster here—they're aboard for this inquiry, and not for duty. Have them bring some more chairs."

Waiting, he walked to the porthole nearest him, and looked at a gray sea running restlessly under the sullen sky. The rain had stopped, and the fog was broken. It drifted, now, in scattered ghostly patches that hugged the shifting hollows. The swells were high, and the *Consolation* rolled creakingly.

Vince became conscious of perfume, subtle and near. He thought of Admiral Wetherbee's logbook, and turned to find Barbara West at his side. She had managed to get luggage sent from the hotel before the *Consolation* sailed, and now she wore a yachting costume of blue skirt and red tailored jacket with exaggerated brass buttons. Vince would have guessed that this shade of red had been especially created to match her lipstick.

"Yes, Miss West?"

"My father doesn't feel well, doctor." She inclined her head slightly toward one of the bunks. Mike Way and the two corpsmen were bringing in chairs, and everybody but Martin West was sitting down. He lay in a lower bunk, his eyes closed and a faintly green cast to his broad face. Martin West built ships, but he couldn't sail in them.

"I wonder if you'd mind excusing us?" the girl went on. "I've told you all I know, and Father doesn't know any more. It was a silly thing, our being forced to come on this ship in the first place!"

Vince manfully put down the anger that rose within him. "I'm sorry, Miss West. For your father, too. But, unfortunately, medical science has discovered no cure for seasickness. He can lie here, and he'll be no more miserable than in his room. Please take your seat."

Her eyes flashed at him in evidence of quick temper. She turned and clicked her heels across the deck. Vince beckoned to Evelyn Brill.

"You've had stenographic training," he said. "Please take notes on all that is said and done here. You may use this pad of temperature charts for the present."

Lieutenant Brill shifted anxiously in his chair. "Doctor," he began, "have you heard anything? I—I overslept, and—"

"Yes," Vince said. "I made my call on the captain just before coming in here, and I saw the latest radio dispatch. The divers are still having trouble trying to secure the downhaul cable. But the men in the *Starfish* told the *Algonquin*, by hull tapping, that they're all right. They have enough food, air and water for several days."

A spasm ran across young Thorpe's thin face. Brill drew a deep breath. "Of course," he said, as if trying to convince himself. "Of course. I ordered those emergency tanks filled. The water will taste, though. It always does, in new tanks. And they have canned rations, and enough soda lime to fight the CO_2. They can always put on the Momsen lungs . . ."

His voice trailed off. Foster Bedell rubbed his newly shaven chin and said, "I'm sure they'll all be saved. And you'll be glad to know that the Navy has approved Mr. West's offer to have the *Westsal* steam to the scene. She's very well equipped with diving and salvage rigs."

Bedell had slept, but his dark eyes still showed red splotches at their corners, and a nervousness lay in the lines of his lean, intense face. From his bunk, Martin West groaned, and Vince Ayres cleared his throat, anxious to get the inquiry under way.

"We're going to resume where we left off this morning," he said. "I'll talk to you, one at a time, in the nurse's office. I want all of you to remember that so far no one is accused, but that each and every one of you—of us—may be under suspicion. Because," and he paused for emphasis, "it is almost a certainty that the murderer of Lieutenant McQuaid is in this room!"

The nurse's office was a small, glass-enclosed room in one corner of the ward. Vince hoped for a psychological effect here; those who waited outside could see the questioning, but unless voices were loud, they could hear nothing through the glass.

He beckoned to John Thorpe. "All right, Thorpe—we'll start with you again. Come on in."

The door opened on the passageway, and an officer entered, followed by the chief master-at-arms of the *Consolation*—a chief boatswain's mate who wore a duty belt and star. Vince looked up inquiringly.

"Sorry, Dr. Ayres," the officer said, and hesitated. Then, crisply: "The Captain has just received radio orders from the District Commandant. To arrest and detain Lieutenant Brill . . ."

7
THREE MINUTES TO KILL . . .

Evelyn Brill stifled a little cry. She dropped the fountain pen she was holding, and it rolled eccentrically with the lift and fall of the ship. Everett Brill sat as if frozen, his face gone gray, for a space. Then he rose, squaring his stocky shoulders.

"Lead the way, please," he said with dignity.

Mike Way retrieved the pen as the door closed on a silence. He whispered, "Don't worry, Miss Brill!" and handed it to her. Vince waited until she had gone into the nurse's office, and then he and young Thorpe followed.

"Sit down," Vince said. "Now, Thorpe, this is what we know: McQuaid was beaten to death somewhere around midnight. The slayer apparently wrapped his weapon in Miss Brill's cape, which was found lying in the rain, on the balcony. The window was open. The murderer may have escaped that way—may have entered from the outside, too, for all we know. Or, the open window may have been a ruse."

"I don't know anything about it, sir," Thorpe said in a high, edged voice. A boy's voice, scarcely changed.

"You were brought in a little while later by the master-at-arms and the night watchman. You had been carrying a broken billiard cue. I'm having that cue examined in the laboratory, Thorpe. Can you remember, now, what you were doing with it?"

Thorpe swallowed, and his face worked. "No, sir! I don't remember anything—not anything. Not till they hit me!"

He rolled his white hat, hoop fashion, between trembling hands The stenciled name was plainly visible on the inner side of its turned-up brim. THORPE, JOHN. He looked dangerously near hysteria.

"The billiard cue," Vince said softly, "would have been capable of breaking a man's skull."

"I didn't do it!" the boy moaned. "I guess—I guess I must have been walking in my sleep!"

Vince Ayres exchanged surprised glances with Evelyn, and was silent while her pen scratched over the temperature chart. He remembered that Barbara West had seen Thorpe pass through the reception room—she had said the sailor looked dazed. It was quite possible, the doctor thought, that the shock of Thorpe's submarine experience could have produced a mental condition that might result in somnambulism. It would take time to check on this.

But could a man commit murder in his sleep?

"Thorpe," he said, "you didn't like Mr. McQuaid. He'd put you on the report. Twice. Did you hold that as a grudge?"

The sailor sprang to his feet, and his voice was loud enough for those outside to hear.

"I didn't have near as big a grudge against him as the skipper!" he blurted. "Mr. McQuaid was going to accuse the captain of being drunk!"

Vince avoided Evelyn's eyes. He looked through the glass, and saw those in the ward react. Mike Way stiffened, and muttered something, and Barbara West's eyebrows went up in thin lines as she met Melhorne's pale gaze. This, he realized with an acute sense of shock, was the best motive for murder so far advanced. . . .

"We don't want any hearsay testimony, Thorpe," he said quietly. "What do you know of this first-hand? Sit down and talk calmly, now. We want the truth—the facts."

"I heard him ask Captain Brill if he was all right," said the sailor. "I could smell the Captain's breath, too. It smelled like alcohol. The Captain got kind of sore, and told Mr. McQuaid to get aft. And then"—he raised his eyes defiantly—"then I saw the captain take a drink out of a bottle. Later—after it—after it happened—Mr. McQuaid kept mumbling about the smell."

"Did you ever walk in your sleep as a child?"

"Why, I—I don't know, sir. I guess not."

"That's all, Thorpe. You'd best not talk to the others about this. You're at liberty for the time being. Who's your roommate?"

"Wop, sir—Cardoni."

"Don't say anything to him, either, just now. That's all."

Thorpe closed the door. Evelyn said, "It looks bad for Dad, Vince! If even the enlisted men thought he was drinking . . ."

"You keep your chin up, young lady," Vince said. "I'm going to have a talk with your father later. There's something we don't know going on here. That arrest—the evidence might warrant arresting Thorpe, but not your father. I can't understand the order from shore. Unless they found something at the hospital—"

"The murder weapon!" Evelyn said. "Maybe that's it."

"Maybe. Well, we know he didn't do it. So keep brave."

She met his eyes, and managed a smile. "Well," she asked, "who'll be next?"

Vince consulted his watch. "We've time for one more before lunch. After that, I want to radio a man I know in Intelligence, to see if he can help. Meanwhile, batten down the hatches for a storm. We're going to talk to Miss Barbara West!"

She entered with haughty defiance and took her seat with an air of utter boredom. She said, "Dr. Ayres, in spite of the wish of my father and myself to help in every way, this is silly! You have no right to cross examine me, and I've nothing to tell you."

"It might come to the point of criminal court proceedings and front page publicity—unless you cooperate now," Vince warned. He studied her for a moment. "Were you acquainted with McQuaid, Miss West?"

The girl hesitated. "Why, I knew him, yes. I know most of the Navy set. Father's business has always been connected with the Navy."

"You'll pardon me for asking personal questions, I hope. Did you ever go out with him, or was he a mere acquaintance?"

She looked at her shoes. "He escorted me to a dance or two. That was nearly two years ago. I hadn't seen him in months."

Vince thoughtfully wiped his glasses. Nothing here to provide even the shadow of a motive from the angle of jealousy, on the basis of what he had been able to learn so far. He rose and paced the room; he looked outside and saw the others sitting in attitudes of impatience. Both Foster Bedell and Victor Melhorne were watching the office. The two hospital corpsmen and a pair of the submarine men—Cardoni and the curly-headed Kowalski—had produced a deck of cards from some place, and were shuffling them to play on the deck.

"What," Vince shot suddenly at the girl, "were you doing on the balcony last night?"

Her dark eyes blazed. "I've told you I wasn't! Just because Admiral Wetherbee says he smelled perfume—"

"And saw the silhouette of a woman, and heard high heels clicking," Vince added. "I might remind you that the Admiral has a mania for detail and a greatly developed faculty for observation. His log, and his testimony will figure importantly in this case. It was after visiting hours. No other woman dressed as you were was on the station."

"I tell you it wasn't I!"

Vince took another tack. "Your father stands to make a great deal of money, if he builds twenty more submarines for the Navy. By the same token, he stands to lose a great deal—millions—if he loses that contract."

The girl stiffened. "What are you driving at, now?"

"It's up to me to examine all possible and probable motives for this murder. If Lieutenant McQuaid alone knew of some fault in the *Starfish's* construction—something that sent her to the bottom—it would be unfortunate for Westco when he regained consciousness and talked."

"Why, you're virtually accusing Father! You—"

Vince smiled grimly. "Not exactly. Remember, I said possible and probable motives. Your father isn't alone in his interest in those new submarines. There are, for instance, Mr. Bedell and Mr. Melhorne."

"That's all crazy!" Barbara West declared. She fidgeted on the edge of her chair. "Suppose there were a flaw in the ship. It'd be found, wouldn't it? They'll raise her."

"Maybe not for some time," Vince said. "Not if the Fleet is ordered to the Atlantic, as it expects to be. No, there might be ample time to fulfill that contract, the way shipbuilding is being rushed today."

"I've told you all I know," the girl insisted. "I saw that sailor—Thorpe—leave. And he was found with that club. I don't see what more evidence you need."

Vince resumed his pacing. "Miss West," he said, "it's very important that we know just where everybody was at the approximate time of the murder, and just before it took place. Look at this—it's a diagram of S.O.Q."

He took a sheet of paper from the desk and handed it to the girl. Her hands were trembling, but he told himself anger was the only emotion he had been able to arouse in her so far. And making her angry wouldn't help. . . .

"It would have been easy for anybody in the odd numbered quiet rooms to open a window, step out on the balcony, and go to Mc-Quaid's room—Number Five," he went on. "The Admiral was in One. He couldn't get out of bed. Number Three was vacant. Lieutenant Brill was in Seven. We know a corpsman saw him in bed at the time—the Lieutenant asked for some three-minute eggs."

Barbara West flashed a feline look at Evelyn. "Three minutes," she drawled, "is just about enough time to kill a man!"

"Perhaps," said Vince. "But we know he was there. Melhorne was in Nine. Nobody went to answer his bell—he didn't ring, the way Lieutenant Brill did. So, we don't know that Melhorne was in his room. He might—"

"Mr. Melhorne was asleep!" Barbara West said quickly.

Vince straightened, and there was a peculiar glint behind his crystal clear glasses. He turned his long, sensitive face toward Evelyn Brill, and said:

"I wanted to be sure of that, Miss West, so that there'd be no need of going farther into that line of inquiry. It'll help if you explain, now, why you went out on the balcony."

"All right!" the dark-haired girl said suddenly. She took a cigarette case from her bag, fumbled at it, and finally got a cigarette between her lips. Vince lighted it for her. She said, "Oh, I haven't anything to hide—there's nothing to be ashamed of. I went out there—yes. To the far end of the balcony, where Mr. Melhorne's room was."

"Why?" Vince asked unmercifully.

"To tell Victor—Mr. Melhorne—that Father had changed his mind. That we were going to the hotel, after all."

"Why didn't Mr. West go?"

"I—I also wanted to tell Victor good night."

Vince said, "Oh. Go on."

"But that's all. Oh, yes—the cape. It was raining, and I saw the nurse's cape lying on a chair. I threw it over my shoulders to protect my dress."

Vince nodded, and glanced at Evelyn. "Your cape," he said. "Now, you told Mr. Melhorne good night, and then returned to the reception room. You—"

"No," said Barbara West. "That's why I know he was asleep. I couldn't wake him, at the window. I could hear him breathing, but I suppose after—after that previous night in the submarine, he was sleeping too soundly. So I went back."

"You took the cape from the chair," Vince said. "Did you put it back there?"

Barbara West shook her head. "No. I dropped it on the balcony. I was frightened. A man came along with a club. I know, now, who it was, of course. Thorpe. But when I saw him, I ran."

"I see," Vince murmured. He opened a notebook and turned through its leaves for a minute. Then he said, "Miss West, may I ask why you didn't go down the hall to Mr. Melhorne's room?"

The girl colored. "I think I'm entitled to keep my reason for not doing that to myself! I didn't wish anybody to see me. That—that isn't the way it sounds. It happens that Victor and I are engaged. But not even Father knows it, and if I'd gone publicly down the hall, Mr. Bedell and others might—"

"I'm sorry I asked you," Vince said humbly. "I think that will be all, now. Thank you." And, as he opened the door for her: "Will you please tell the others to go to their dinner? We'll muster here again at two o'clock."

He faced Evelyn when they were alone. She said, with a sigh, "Well, Vince . . . are we getting anywhere?"

"I don't know. I know this: Miss West hasn't really told everything. Either that, or the Admiral's log is off, and, knowing the Admiral, I don't think the latter is true. You heard her say she saw the man with the club on the balcony. Well, the Admiral's log puts her there at 'about 2310.' That's ten minutes past eleven. And he puts the man with 'a swab handle, or something heavier' there at 2330—half past eleven."

Evelyn frowned. "The Admiral might have made an error in his time."

"Possibly. But he's spent a lifetime moving on schedule, being on time to the minute. And when a man lies awake nights writing inconsequential things in a logbook, he's apt to be fussy about any facts."

"What do you think, Vince? About Thorpe?"

"I don't know," he confessed. "I must go by the laboratory and see what they found on the billiard cue. Nobody would pick Thorpe as a murderer—he's more the bewildered boy type. No, I think what Miss West revealed is more important."

"What made you so sure—about her and Melhorne, I mean?"

He sat on a corner of the desk, lighting a cigarette and grinning through the smoke. "I wasn't sure. But did you ever see colder eyes in a man? And they only warm up a little when he's looking at that girl. So I figured this might be the old set-up—right hand man of the boss in love with the boss's daughter. I knew from the Admiral's observations that she was out on that balcony, and it wasn't likely that she went out there to see any of the others. So I dropped a hint that Melhorne might be accused, and she rose to the bait. Protective instinct—it's strong, in all women."

"But what do you think she hasn't told?"

"Maybe not everything about her association with McQuaid. Maybe there was something to make Melhorne jealous. And she hasn't told everything about that man with the club. I'm sure of that. Oh, she saw him, all right. In the rain and the semi-darkness, one man would look very much like another. Now, suppose she saw him come through Melhorne's window after she left it? It wouldn't have to be Melhorne—he might have been sleeping so soundly anybody could come through his room. But Barbara West would be afraid it was Melhorne. The protective instinct comes to the fore. She actually didn't have to tell us anything, but she didn't know how much we knew—and she decided to establish an alibi for him. So, she says he was fast asleep. But the time element doesn't jibe. She and the Admiral may have seen two different persons."

"One of them Thorpe," Evelyn said.

"Exactly. And the other—the murderer!"

RADIO USS CONSOLATION ELEVENTH 1242 BT
PRIORITY TO COMMANDANT NINETEENTH NA-
VAL CONSOLATION ANCHORED AT SCENE STAR-
FISH SALVAGE OPERATIONS 1239. STANDING BY.
MCKEE.
TOD 1251.

8
ABOUT THAT BOTTLE

The old navy custom of a brisk walk on the quarterdeck after the midday meal sent Vince Ayres topside. A man could think better up here, too. But there was the distraction of the *Algonquin*, tossing on the swells less than a quarter of a mile away, her small, cluttered deck showing a bustle of activity. She put out a motor sailer, and two stretcher cases were taken aboard the hospital ship. Divers—suffering from the bends despite hours in the salvage tug's recompression chamber.

Vince watched them grimly, remembering that Mike Way wanted to dive. A shadow fell across the rail, and he looked up to see the big, ugly chief.

Mike Way saluted. "Doctor, sir," he began, "I thought maybe you'd be wanting to talk to the Captain. I heard what Thorpe said—about him drinking."

"Yes," Vince nodded. "I'm going to ask him a few questions."

"Could I go along, sir? I know a little—about that bottle."

Vince turned toward the hatch. "No time like now, Chief. Come on."

They descended two ladders. Vince said: "I haven't had an opportunity to discuss this thing with you. But I'd like to know something about the feuds—the grudges—that seemed to exist on the *Starfish*. I know about Thorpe and McQuaid, of course. What were the others?"

Mike Way's blue eyes were honest. He said, "Well, of course Mr. McQuaid was sore at the Captain. But that would have wore off. The Captain may not wear an Academy ring, sir, but he's a real skipper if there ever was one, and he'd have had Mr. McQuaid eating out of his hand in another couple of weeks—and liking it."

"Go on," Vince said.

"That's all, doctor. Except Cardoni. I wouldn't call that a grudge—Cardoni was out of his head when he took that poke at Mr. McQuaid. He'd have realized in a little while that the Lieutenant was only doing his duty when he shut that door. If he'd been another minute doing it, the water would have been coming into the control room until all hell wouldn't have stopped it—and none of us would be here."

"How about the two civilians—Bedell and Melhorne? Any resentment toward McQuaid, or anybody else, shown by them while they were on the bottom?"

"No, sir," Mike Way said positively. "They acted like white men. All the way through."

The pair came to Everett Brill's room. A sailor wearing a duty belt was stationed outside—the *Consolation* carried no marines—and even before the sentry had unlocked the door Vince could hear Brill's caged, restless pacing. The submarine commander turned quickly as they entered. His iron gray head thrust forward, and hope leaped into his eyes.

Vince said, "There's no word, yet, Lieutenant. They're still working. I came down to ask you a few questions."

"If I could just be down there with them!" Brill said brokenly. "If I could help, some way! I thought perhaps they'd let me go over to the *Algonquin*, and—"

He spread his hands helplessly, but he began talking again before Vince could say anything. "Why am I under arrest, doctor? Regulations say an officer must be informed of the charges against him. *Are* there any charges?"

"I don't know any more than you do," Vince said. "Just that the order came from the commandant of Nineteenth Naval District."

"If it's because of the murder," Brill declared, "that's one thing—and if it's because I lost the *Starfish*, that's another. I've got a right to know!"

It was easy to see that he considered a murder charge trivial compared to an accusation of negligence in the submarine disaster. He was still a dazed, harried man; Vince had seen that expression on the faces of Navy fighters who were down on one knee while the referee's arm swung. . . .

"Lieutenant," he said, "I have to ask you some questions that bear on the McQuaid killing. They go back to the *Starfish*, however. I've learned that McQuaid apparently had some sort of row with you, and that he entertained the idea you'd been drinking."

Brill stiffened. "That was between Mr. McQuaid and myself. There was friction, yes."

"But the suspicion that you were intoxicated . . . ?"

"I wasn't, of course," Brill snapped. Then he smiled without mirth. "It was a silly thing, and could have been explained in a minute—if I hadn't been bullheaded enough to believe that no junior officer was entitled to an explanation! I had a bad cough, as you know. The pharmacist's mate had fixed me some cough medicine. Let's see—terpin— terpin, something."

"Elixir of terpin hydrate?"

"That was it. I wanted to carry the bottle in my pocket, so I poured it into a small flask—a flat, half-pint bottle. There was no label on the bottle, doctor, but that was nobody's business, either. I guess the stuff has a pretty high alcoholic content. Enough to smell. The odor is something like liquor—or, rather, like a liqueur."

"That's true," Vince said. "The pharmacist's mate could have explained."

"He's—one of those men caught aft," Brill said, and once more the *Starfish* and her men outweighed everything else in his mind. "For a long time I hoped that they—some of them, anyway—had been able to get into the after torpedo room and block off the water, as we did forward. But we tapped on the bulkhead, and there was no answer. . . ."

Mike Way broke the grim silence. "I took that bottle out of the captain's pocket, sir. When we hoisted him up the hatch. I thought—"

"Look here, Chief!" Brill exclaimed. "Are you the man who struck me there in the darkness?"

The torpedoman grinned his hearty approval of that blow, but shook his head. "No, sir. I don't know who did that, Captain. But I took the bottle, and dropped it behind the torpedo rack. That's one reason I'd like to dive, Dr. Ayres. I want to get that downhaul cable secured, and I want to tell the crew of the rescue bell to have somebody bring up that bottle!"

"You'll wait," Vince said grimly. "There are other divers in the outfit. Well, Lieutenant, that's all I have to bother you with, just now. I might ask you the one question we are all asking. Have you any idea who might have had reason to kill McQuaid?"

Brill looked at him squarely. "I have not, doctor. I can't conceive of anybody—any man who was in my ship—dreaming of doing such a thing. And I can see no reason for it."

As Vince and Mike Way climbed the ladders, the big chief swore softly. "Of all the dumb tricks!" he exclaimed. "I thought I was doing the skipper a favor by ditching that bottle. I knew Mr. McQuaid had out the old squirrel rifle for him, and he looked kind of red in the face, and—"

"I understand," Vince said as the chief halted lamely. There was a loyalty here that transcended rank; it played a large part in making the Navy what it was, because the Navy was full of officers deserving such loyalty. And, Vince thought, Everett Brill was one of them. "It was a fever, Chief. He was ill, not drunk. He should have turned in on the sick list instead of taking that ship out for trials."

But there was the testimony young John Thorpe would give to the board investigating the *Starfish* disaster. "I saw the captain drinking from a bottle. . . ."

Whether he had been placed in custody because of the murder or because of the loss of his ship, Brill was in a tight spot.

RADIO USS CONSOLATION ELEVENTH 1350 BT
SIMMONS INTELLIGENCE NINETEENTH NAVAL BT
PLEASE CHECK FINANCIAL STATUS WESTCO
IRON WORKS AND PROVIDE ANY INFORMATION
POSSIBLE ON VICTOR MELHORNE AND FOSTER
BEDELL OF THAT FIRM. BT
VINCE AYRES.
TOD 1358

The afternoon seemed wasted so far as Vince's questioning was concerned, but Admiral Wetherbee—Vince made up his mind he'd visit the old sea dog later in the day—sent in a copy of the latest entry in his log. And this offered the only seemingly logical explanation of a matter that had been puzzling Vince and others.

It happened that he was discussing this phase of the case at the time, while examining Cardoni. The dark-faced machinist's mate was ill at ease, still grief stricken and shocked, and very contrite.

"I know it looks bad for me, doctor," he mumbled. "Jeez! I kept sounding off about how I wished the Lieutenant would check out because—because he was the one that shut that door. But I didn't mean anything. I didn't mean what I said."

"I understand that, Cardoni," Vince said gravely. He glanced at Evelyn, who was recording the testimony, and suddenly asked: "How's your arm? Did it pain you last night?"

"A little, sir. But they gave me a shot—in the good arm. It hurt, some, but I slept. I was pooped."

"You slept soundly, then?"

Cardoni looked wary. "I didn't leave my bunk sir, not till they broke us out to say that Mr. McQuaid had been killed."

"You didn't hear anything, or see anybody in the hall? Your door was shut?"

"Yes, sir, it was. I didn't hear a sound. I've been thinking it was funny—me right across the hall from the Lieutenant's room, and not hearing the—whoever it was—slugging him. Before I went to sleep, I heard him mumbling a couple of times. About that smell."

Vince nodded. "By the way, do you remember any unusual smell in the submarine?"

"No, sir. All pigboats smell bad. Maybe the cook was fixing something in the galley, but I don't remember any special smell. I—all of that is sort of like a dream, now, doctor. It's hazy."

The hospital corpsman came in just then and handed Vince a sheet of paper. He looked at it and smiled. The Admiral had sent the logbook itself, last time.

"I wonder if Admiral Wetherbee's making some private entries, to be made public later?" Vince chuckled. "This is just a portion of today's log. All right, Cardoni—that'll do. Let's go out and read this to everybody, Miss Brill."

Barbara West's expression was scornful when Vince announced that he had more notes from the Admiral's log. It was Melhorne's turn to look as bored as his pale eyes would allow. Foster Bedell was sitting as if asleep, his eyes closed, but he came respectfully to an attentive posture, and the enlisted men stopped their card playing to listen.

0930 Proceeding to scene of salvage operations. Navigator on bridge, standard speed. Wind, Force Five, Sea moderate. Starboard leg in dry-dock as before.

1000 Proceeding with murder investigation. Dispatched urgent priority radio messages Nineteenth Naval.

1029 Understand, now, why murder blows were not heard. Must question CARDONI. Perhaps he remembers now what took place as submarine went down by stern. Must examine Captain's log of STARFISH. The reason—

Cardoni interrupted. "I can't tell the Admiral anything doctor!" And Barbara West fumed: "Isn't this a lot of drivel, Dr. Ayres? I'm sure all of us would like to get to the bottom of this affair, but it appears to me that this so-called log is nothing more than the musings of a meddling old man!"

Vince silenced her with a look. He said, "Please listen to this. I think you'll agree that it's an instance of very shrewd deduction—"

The reason nobody heard murderer's blows may be accounted for by the possibility that they were synchronized exactly to the blows of the hospital corpsman who was chopping ice for Lieut. McQUAID'S ice cap, in the adjacent diet kitchen. This was at approximately 2356. . . .

9
THE OLD MAN MEDDLES

Evelyn Brill left her father's room with a feeling of desperate hope-lessness. Lieutenant Brill's mental attitude showed in every line of his weathered face and in the beaten slump of his shoulders and it was infectious. That other time—after the collision when he was executive officer in the *Bolton*—he was still a fighter, and his determination to win against the charges, Evelyn thought, had been mainly responsible for his winning.

She knew that Everett Brill, fighting to keep bright a name that had been on Navy rolls for a long time. This one was a stranger. Twenty-five men remained entombed alive on the sea's bottom, and their skipper had left his courage with them in the cold, stinking torpedo room. With every hour, he had grown more certain that his arrest had nothing to do with the murder . . . they were holding him responsible, he said, for the loss of his ship. For her loss, and the deaths of the men in the after-compartments.

Nothing could cheer him. Evelyn forced a parting smile, kissed the tip of his ear, and went topside on her way to the nurses' quarters. A girl couldn't be Navy always. Sometimes you had to cry. . . .

She saw Big Mike leaning on the rail, yonder, watching the *Algonquin* in the fading twilight. And Barbara West came out on deck wearing a dark, fur-trimmed frock smart enough for evening, and leaving that subtle perfume in her wake. She didn't see Evelyn, but went toward the rail where the chief torpedoman stood. She walked with a slinky gait. Predatory, the girl who had to wear plain white drill told herself—and went to her room hating Barbara at the moment.

Mae Kennedy was at Evelyn's door. She was plump, and some-thing about her inspired delirious sailors to clasp her hand and mut-ter "Mother!" And just now she looked as miserable as Evelyn felt.

"I'm—I'm going to be very ill!" she moaned. "Before I die, I want to tell you—the Admiral—wants to see you—"

She lurched for her room across the passageway as the *Consola-tion* rolled. "Right away!" she gasped, and vanished inside.

Evelyn smiled, despite herself. At least, she had been spared sea-sickness. She gathered up the notes she had taken on the tempera-ture charts, and went to the Admiral's room.

He called, "Come in!" and a corpsman left the room with his supper tray. It contained, Evelyn noted, the remains of the inevitable turkey leg. Admiral Wetherbee waved to a chair.

"Wonderful to be at sea again!" he boomed. "If I could only take a turn or two around deck! The doctor told me that I might be trans-ferred to the mechanized forces tomorrow."

"Mechanized forces?" Evelyn said.

"Yes—the wheelchair brigade," he chuckled. Then, soberly, "How's your father?"

Evelyn told him, and there was a strange glint under his shaggy brows.

"Just like the Navy. Keeps a man on pins and needles, never tell-ing him what his next tour of duty will be till the last minute. Then it's something he doesn't want."

"I almost hate it!" Evelyn said in a cold, flat tone. "If Dad gets . . . beached, I'll resign. I'll take up nursing on the Outside!"

"H'm," said Admiral Wetherbee. "I expected you to turn to the Outside, some day—but not as a civilian. No. I was quite sure you'd be a Navy wife."

"I'll never marry a Navy man! I won't sit home worrying and wait-ing. Like the families of those men in the *Starfish*! As my mother used to do. I'd want a home. Not here today and gone tomorrow, but one home—for always!"

She got restlessly from the chair and looked out of the porthole. Full darkness lay on the sea, but the *Algonquin's* lights rode the swells over yonder, and she could see masthead blinkers winking on a destroyer which was standing by beyond. There were Navy men on the *Algonquin* who hadn't given up fighting—men brave beyond the line of duty each time they volunteered to dive two hundred and forty feet down, under that rolling, shifting pressure.

The Admiral said, softly, "They brought three more of them aboard this evening, Evelyn. Yes . . . there are easier ways of making a living than being in the Navy! Sit down. I sent for you because I wanted to talk about the murder."

Evelyn obeyed. "We don't seem to be getting anywhere," she sighed. "Evidence points to Thorpe, but it couldn't have been that boy!"

"Anything's possible in a case like this," said the Admiral. "But I'm inclined to agree with you. Not because young Thorpe wouldn't be capable of murder—I haven't more than had a glimpse or two at him, you understand, but psychologists say that all of us are potentially capable of killing. The reason I don't think it was Thorpe is because the person who murdered McQuaid was a colder, shrewder, more calculating type. An older person."

"Whom do you suspect?"

The Admiral shook his head, "They're too many to enumerate, right now. But I'm afraid we haven't seen the last of it. I wanted to warn you to be very careful. Lock your door, and keep a sharp lookout at all times. Don't go out on deck after dark."

"You mean—"

There was a knock at the door. The Admiral lowered his voice. "The murderer is still a shipmate of ours," he said. "Come in!"

It was Vince Ayres. The light glinted from his glasses. His long face was grave and pale. Evelyn rose slowly, an unasked question in her eyes.

"Mike Way," Vince said. "He's disappeared!"

It took a minute for the full significance of these words to make itself felt. Evelyn was dimly conscious of the deck's lift and fall; two successive swells rolled beneath the *Consolation*, and she thought: *Men disappear only in one way at sea!*

A sharp picture unrolled before her like a movie flash-back. Mike Way's silhouette against the twilight sky and the tossing sea, and Barbara West's slinking approach behind his back. She tried to shut her mind against this before it went on, into a scene of her mind's own invention. . . .

Vince was talking. "—at supper, all right. But I had the word passed for him, and no luck. Then I called on the master-at-arms force. They searched all the way down to the double bottoms. He isn't aboard."

"Did you report this to Captain McKee?" asked the Admiral.

Vince nodded. "I had to. They turned searchlights on the water, but didn't find anything. Then—" he bit his lip "—a seaman found his cap on deck. Forward. The way this sea is running, if a man fell over the side, he'd have to be a pretty good swimmer to keep afloat very long."

He was breaking things gradually, Evelyn realized. Out of consideration for her. Vince knew that Mike Way practically worshiped the deck Everett Brill walked on, and that if Brill were accused in the loss of his ship, Mike's testimony might prove of great value. The big chief torpedoman had been in the control room when the *Starfish* made her trial dives. . . .

The Admiral rumbled, "It's not likely he *fell* over. I'd just reminded Evelyn that we still are shipmates with a murderer. And it's my belief, doctor, that the killer will strike again. Young lady, let me see the notes you took today."

He skimmed through them rapidly, turning back now and then to read some passages twice. The girl and Vince Ayres sat in silence. Evelyn told herself it was impossible for Barbara West to have been responsible for Mike Way's disappearance. Oh, a child might be able to push a man over the side, but a man as big and strong as Mike Way would have to be unconscious before he hit the water, else—

"It doesn't tie in!" the Admiral complained. "It might have, a little bit, until this latest incident came along. Way wasn't one of the men who could have known what happened aft in the *Starfish*, like Mc-Quaid—he thought, instead, that there's no better skipper in the Navy."

"Nothing ties in," Vince said bitterly. A sudden thought struck him. "Unless Mike Way discovered something we don't know about—unless he stumbled onto something just tonight, and the murderer knew it!"

A pharmacist's mate who wore a white laboratory apron looked in the door, saw Vince Ayres, and entered.

"Excuse me, Dr. Ayres," he said. "We've finished the microscopic and chemical examination of that billiard cue. Apparently the rain washed away practically everything, but—"

Vince was impatient. "But what?"

"There is an unmistakable trace of blood, sir, on the cue's heavy end!"

Vince looked quickly at the other two. Evelyn said, "That boy?" and the Admiral frowned quizzically.

"Very well," Vince said slowly. "Thank you. And you will please make a written report of your findings, but keep it secret."

"Aye, aye, sir."

Admiral Wetherbee looked up when the man had gone. "There's enough circumstantial evidence, of course, to hang young Thorpe. But circumstantial evidence isn't enough, and I'm against it. You're a doctor. You saw McQuaid. Could that billiard cue have been the murder weapon?"

"If enough blows were struck, I think it could have," Vince said. "My impression would be that something heavier was used. Unfortunately, I didn't have time to make a more thorough examination."

"There'll be a post-mortem at the hospital, of course," the Admiral said. "Now, you've questioned Thorpe and had an opportunity to observe him. What do you think?"

"You know his type, Admiral. They join the Navy too young to adjust themselves to a man's outfit. They're the ones who get most of the inaptitude discharges. Thorpe probably was something of a mamma's boy on the Outside; he undoubtedly came in for a lot of razzing and horseplay in the Navy. Add to that the very severe nervous shock suffered in the *Starfish*, and you have a person who might well develop a complex, or a fixation. But, in Thorpe's case, you'd scarcely expect it to find an outlet in murder!"

The Admiral nodded. "Are you going to have him thrown in the brig?"

"What good would that do?" asked Vince. "He can't very well get away. I'd like to watch him for the present."

Evelyn left presently, and Vince Ayres walked down the passageway with her, turning aside to go to the radio room. As they parted, he caught her hand and squeezed it briefly.

"Tired?" he asked.

"A little. It seems ten years since—since all this began to happen."

"I know it does. Evelyn, you're dead game. But you're too lovely—too sweet—to be in any place where you can get mixed up in such a tragic mess! After it's all cleared up, I—"

She interrupted. "Good night, Vince. Will you let me know if they find out anything—about Mike Way, I mean?"

"Of course," he said huskily, and looked after her with a strange expression. She locked the door of her room, and for a long while she leaned by the porthole, watching the *Algonquin's* lights. Signal blinkers were going, like fireflies caught at the masthead, and she could see the faint stirring of men on deck. Still diving, she thought, and a sense of the passage of time struck her with a sudden pang.

Those men in the *Starfish* had been waiting nearly sixty hours.

RADIO USS CONSOLATION ELEVENTH 2105 BT
SIMMONS INTELLIGENCE NINETEENTH NAVAL BT
IMPORTANT PLEASE QUESTION MCCARTHY
NIGHT WATCHMAN ABOUT ENCOUNTER WITH
THORPE NIGHT OF MURDER. MUST BE SURE
WHAT WEAPON HE USED CLUBBING THORPE BT
VINCE AYRES.
TOD 2115.

10
PROWLER ON THE DECK

Captain McKee of the *Consolation* sent for Vince. He was a medical corps officer, but in spite of the oak leaves on his sleeves instead of stars, no more military-looking line officer could have been found afloat. As it was, navigational duties and the responsibility for the operation of the ship fell upon a line officer of commander's rank.

The tall, erect doctor was at his desk when Vince entered, and he stood on no military ceremony now. He motioned to a chair and offered Vince a cigar.

"This chief who disappeared," he began. "Way. A very good man, I understand."

"Yes, sir," Vince said. There was a saying that chief petty officers were the backbone of the Navy. It applied, Vince thought, to the brass-buttoned men of Mike Way's caliber.

"He had something like twelve years' service," the Captain went on. "He was a master diver. Record—I have it here—is perfect. Cited for bravery over and beyond the line of duty in diving to recover the bodies of five men killed in the crash of a PB-Y plane. Cited for heroism in the rescue of a seaman who fell overboard from the destroyer *Bolton*."

"I didn't know about that, sir," Vince said. "And I had him for a patient once—with the bends. He was modest."

He wondered what Captain McKee was getting at. The Captain rose and paced thoughtfully across the deck.

"It would be a shame to spoil such a record, wouldn't it? I mean, if, technically, the Chief had deserted—or jumped ship."

"I don't understand," Vince said. "Do you mean—"

"I mean," McKee smiled, "that Chief Mike Way isn't lost at sea at all. No, by golly, and I don't think a man with his courage and stamina ever will be! He merely swam over to the *Algonquin*—he reported aboard and asked permission to be allowed to dive!"

"Why, the big damned fool!" Vince exclaimed. "With those ribs of his! He kept asking me if I could fix up a transfer, and I put him off—I told him to wait."

Captain McKee nodded grimly. "And it's hard to wait while your shipmates are on the bottom. It was too hard for Mike Way. Well, he's over there, now. The captain of the *Algonquin* reported a little while ago. And I'm wondering what to do."

Vince shook his head. "Well, if a man can swim a quarter of a mile—"

"That's what I thought. By golly, if the medical officer in the *Algonquin* will let him dive, why should we put a red mark on a record like his? I wanted to ask you—you're in charge of this murder inquiry. Do you need Way?"

"No," Vince said. He smiled, picturing the surprise on the salvage tug when the big, ugly diver came splashing alongside and called for a line. "No, sir. I may have to ask him some questions later, but they can wait. And I hope he's lucky!"

"I hope," Captain McKee said fervently, "that God's holding on to his lifeline when he's forty fathoms down!"

Vince called Evelyn Brill on her room telephone, and told her the good news. He heard the quick, joyous catch of her breath, and a sound suspiciously like sobbing. He laughed, and said: "Now you can sleep, Evelyn. And I've got a hunch that things are going to break for us—that this mess will be straightened out."

She was her father's daughter. She said, "If anybody can secure that downhaul cable in a sea like this, it's Mike Way!"

For a long time after Vince called her, she stood at the porthole in her room and watched the dark sea run under the moon. Swells rolled rhythmically along the side of the ship: they might have been melody transmuted to liquid and touched lightly by the moon sparkle—a melody to which the ship danced. This fancy was a soothing thought to dwell upon, and Evelyn tried to pick out the three-quarter beat of a waltz as she watched the surging roll.

But the sea was faster, more savage. Like a march, she thought. The memories of a dozen Navy parade grounds came back to her. Bands playing, blue-clad men swinging across asphalt with all the reckless, "salty" disdain of the seamen for strict military formations and customs, and a little girl in pigtails watching. Thrilling to *Anchors Aweigh*. The Blue and Gold on parade. . . .

Admiral Wetherbee's dry old voice saying, "Yes . . . there are easier ways of making a living than being in the Navy . . ."

And the tempo of the sea changed. There was a new note in the wild symphony of wind and wave. There were clouds darkening the ringed moon, and the only light came from the *Algonquin* as she pitched out yonder. Evelyn listened to a tympanic clatter that beat with all the insistence of jungle drums against the ship's side. She thrust her head out of the porthole and looked down.

A line, faintly straggling in the gloom, ran from a porthole that was below and forward, and dipped in the sea. The thing that hammered against the hull, the girl decided, must be a bucket. Some member of the *Consolation's* crew was probably intending to wash clothes.

She went to bed. The timpani continued. It was in her ears dimly, like a thing only half remembered, when she fell asleep.

Vince went out on deck for a breath of fresh air. Only the standing lamps were burning, casting their bluish, unreal glow in little circles. A thin scudding of clouds blew across the sky, and shrouded a moon that had a luminous ring around it.

More stormy weather, Vince thought, and watched the lights of a new ship coming up over the rolling swells. Somebody called up to the bridge, and the signalman of the watch answered that she was the *Westsal*—Westco's salvage ship. And then Martin West puffed out on deck, his seasickness past, with Foster Bedell and Victor Melhorne following him respectfully.

They watched from the rail until the *Westsal* had anchored and was swinging with the tide. West said, "I'll want you both over there to direct operations. Those men must be saved, and we've got to get the ship up. Pacific Maritime is probably already trying to move in on the government contracts!"

Melhorne's thin voice said, "If we can get away from this damned murder investigation!" But Foster Bedell was more positive. He said, quietly, "I'll go aboard her in the morning, Mr. West."

They turned below, talking earnestly and in a low tone. Vince lighted the cigar Captain McKee had given him, and watched the dark, swinging rush of the water by the ship's side. Anything to help speed the rescue of those twenty-five men in the *Starfish*—if Melhorne and Bedell were needed to direct the salvage operations on the civilian ship, the murder inquiry could wait.

He heard a light footfall across the deck, and turned casually. What he saw brought him around, watching tensely.

A man in pajamas and a Navy white hat—a barefoot man—was walking yonder with a strange, mechanical gait, his hands thrust before him. John Thorpe!

In that instant, the danger of the lad's going over the side struck Vince Ayres, and he was torn between the wish to watch Thorpe for a minute and the wisdom of seizing him immediately. He started softly across the deck, and Thorpe saved him from having to make a decision. Thorpe turned and entered the passageway that led between two of the wards.

Vince Ayres followed. It was after taps, and the lights were dim. Nobody else was stirring. Thorpe came to a ladder leading to the deck below, and went part of the way down it.

The hand chains rattled, but the young sailor still moved as if he were asleep. From above, Vince could see the stenciled name on the brim of the white hat. THORPE, JOHN . . .

Thorpe turned slowly, and came back up. His eyes, apparently unseeing, looked straight at the doctor. He moved aft along the passageway.

A buzzer sounded, and Vince saw the red light go on above a door. Admiral Wetherbee's door—

A hospital corpsman came from the nurse's office just as Vince passed it. The doctor reached out to catch the corpsman's arm.

"Wait a minute," he whispered. "Wait till this man gets by!"

The surprised corpsman nodded, and just then John Thorpe turned into the Admiral's room.

Swift speculation flashed through Vince's mind as he sprang forward. Could a buzzer and a red light make their impression on the subconsciousness of a sleepwalker, causing him to deviate from his course? Could the loud breathing and the mutterings of a man in a coma have done the same—drawing John Thorpe through that hospital window when he held a potentially murderous club in his hands?

Thorpe had closed the door behind him. Vince opened it quietly. He saw the Admiral, propped up as high as the angle of his hoisted leg would allow, his wide-awake, sea-blue eyes following every move of the sleepwalker.

Admiral Wetherbee put his finger across his lips. Vince nodded, and took up a position by the door. Thorpe went to the bulkhead by the porthole, touched it, and turned. He came back, brushed against the Admiral's bedside table, and halted there. Then he touched the top of the table—and picked, up the Admiral's logbook.

A water glass slid from the table and fell to the deck. Thorpe flinched, then cried out as it struck his bare foot, and looked wildly around him. "Where—what—"

"Easy!" said Vince Ayres. He caught Thorpe's arm and steered him to a chair. "Sit down a minute."

Thorpe was trembling, and there was a sobbing catch to his breath. He moaned, "I did it again! I—I was asleep, doctor! Walking in my sleep again!"

"Looks that way," Vince said. "Just be quiet a minute. You're all right."

Thorpe drew a long, shuddering breath. The Admiral and Vince Ayres looked at each other silently. Vince took the logbook from the sailor's clutching hand, and replaced it on the table.

"What time did you go to bed, Thorpe?" he asked in a kindly tone.

"About nine, I guess, sir."

"Let's see—you have a roommate, haven't you?"

"Yes, sir. Wop—Wop Cardoni, sir. He was already in bed, I guess."

"Don't you know for certain?"

"Well, the light was out, doctor, and I didn't want to wake him. I saw his clothes on the chair."

"Dream anything?" Vince asked.

"No, sir—yes, I did, too! That I was down in the submarine!"

"Will you sound your buzzer again, Admiral?" Vince requested. And, when the corpsman came, "Bring me fifteen grains of sodium bromide. Wait outside, Thorpe, and we'll talk about this tomorrow. I want you to take the sodium bromide and go to bed. This time, lock your door and put the key where you can't possibly get it without waking yourself by the effort."

Thorpe said, "They won't kick me out of the Navy, will they, doctor?"

"Don't worry about that," Vince answered.

"No, sir. Thank you, sir."

The Admiral motioned to the night duty corpsman. "When you come back, Jones, look in the diet kitchen and see if you can find me a cold turkey leg."

The two enlisted men went out; Thorpe was still shaken and dazed. The Admiral looked at Vince Ayres.

"Well?" he inquired.

"If you're asking me whether his somnambulism is real—I don't know. But I'd say that if it isn't, that boy is doing a good job as an actor!"

"I didn't mean that," said the Admiral. "But isn't it rather curious that he should come in here—and especially that he picked up the logbook? That log of mine has some quite valuable data bearing on this murder mystery. I'm wondering if this was an attempt to steal it. That is supposing, of course, that the lad was really awake."

Vince shook himself. "What would be his object in faking?" he demanded. "You heard him ask if he might be kicked out of the Navy. And you know as well as I that a man who walks in his sleep is a risky person to have at sea—no telling when he might walk over the side. Oh, somnambulists do strange things. I've heard of cases where they buried money or valuables, and couldn't remember, later, what they'd done. There was mental quirk, here. Call it a fixation, if you wish—the idea that the money was in danger of being stolen had preyed on the subconscious. Perhaps Thorpe went to sleep thinking about your logbook."

"What sort of tools did the sleepwalkers use for digging when they buried money?" asked Admiral Wetherbee. "Could a man wield a pick, for instance, without waking himself?"

"I don't remember that the case histories related that detail," Vince said. "And I suppose it would depend on the individual as to how soundly he slept. It's rather hard to believe Thorpe could be guilty of murder."

"I don't think he is, myself," the Admiral admitted. "But if a sleepwalker could swing a pick and not know it, he could club a man's skull. Of course, I'm not a medical man. But if there is any sort of thing such as somnambulism in connection with schizophrenia—that's what you call split personality, isn't it?—we'd have a real clue."

Vince shook his head dubiously, and the old man sighed as if disappointed in the failure of medical science to make the tie-in he sought. The Admiral said, "Well, we're becalmed. You'd better turn in, yourself."

Vince said goodnight, and went into the passageway. Thorpe waited for him there, still looking scared, and Vince beckoned him along.

"Show me your room," he told the sailor. "I'll see that you have that sedative, and you see to it that you stay in your bunk."

"Yes, sir," Thorpe answered, and led the way down a ladder.

Above the rattle of the hand chains, Vince heard a rhythmic clanking somewhere against the ship's side. He put this sound out of thought, and watched the bluejacket keenly as they came to the door of a room on the outboard side of the passageway. Thorpe hesitated.

"I don't want to wake up Cardoni, sir," he said as he turned the knob. The light from the passageway widened in the room and fell across the two bunks. Vince Ayres heard a gasp from the boy in front of him, and Thorpe recoiled so suddenly he collided with the doctor.

Wop Cardoni was sitting up in bed, his body at an angle that would have been impossible to maintain without support. His face was contorted and purple. There was a small rope—the Navy called it "line"—tied to the upper bunk. It looped around Cardoni's neck, and then ran out the open porthole. Outside was the clatter against the hull.

"He's—Cardoni's dead!" Thorpe cried.

11
DEATH HARNESSES THE TIDE

The corpsman who came with the sodium bromide had one look at Cardoni before Vince sent him to inform Captain McKee that a new murder had been committed. John Thorpe sank into the room's only chair, resting his elbows on the writing desk and burying his face in shaking hands. There was a crowd gathering in the passageway before Vince had completed his examination, and he heard Captain McKee call, "Gangway! Break it up, you men! All of you get back to your bunks except the master-at-arms force." Then, to Vince: "Is there any chance of resuscitation?"

Vince shook his head. "He's been dead for some time. He was killed in a slow and diabolical fashion—after first having been stunned by a blow on the head. Look here, sir!"

Captain McKee stared as Vince hauled in on the line. Cardoni's body settled back in bed; the line came through the porthole and revealed a bucket tied at the other end.

Vince spilled water out of this and lifted it through the porthole.

"It acted like a sea anchor, Captain," he explained. "Every time a swell ran along the side of the ship, it tightened the line on Cardoni's neck."

The Captain nodded, and bent to examine the strangling loop. "Marlin hitch," he pronounced. "It's used to lash Navy hammocks. Good God! It would decapitate this man, if it had stayed on him long enough!"

Vince leaned wearily against the bulkhead. This matched the horror of McQuaid's murder, back there at the hospital. This was a sample of the terror that had come to sea with the seven men who had already gone through hell at the bottom of the Pacific. Six now, Vince thought, and the significance of this crime struck him all at once.

First, McQuaid. Now, Cardoni. There was only one man left who had been in the after-compartments and who had escaped. That was John Thorpe. . . .

"How can you tell he was hit, first?" the captain was asking.

"He was struck on his forehead," Vince explained. "If you'll look closely, you can see the place despite the general discoloration. What with, I can't say. The bucket, probably."

"There's a broom locker down the passageway," volunteered one of the master-at-arms force. "The bucket belongs there."

"Who found him?" McKee asked.

"We did—Thorpe and I." Vince remembered something, then. He turned on the boy at the desk. "Thorpe, you said you thought Cardoni was asleep, awhile ago. Did you see him in bed?"

"I didn't turn on the light," Thorpe moaned. "I was up on the deck, and when I came down here I undressed in the dark and got in bed. I thought he was asleep, and I guess he was dead all the time. Because I—I heard that bucket banging on the side."

"That was about two hours ago?"

"Yes, sir."

Vince looked at his watch. He could feel Captain McKee's eyes sharply upon him. It was only ten-thirty, now. Two hours ago there had been all kinds of people moving around the ship, topside and below. Mike Way had gone over the side for his swim to the *Algonquin* at perhaps half past seven or eight. Barbara West had been on deck, and later her father had been there with Victor Melhorne and Foster Bedell. Evelyn Brill had been in Admiral Wetherbee's room about two hours ago.

The murder trail here, he thought bitterly, was even colder than the one he had been trying to follow since that rainy midnight at the hospital. Only last midnight, it was, although it seemed an incredibly long time ago. . . .

"If you went to bed," Captain McKee was asking Thorpe, "how did it come that you were with Dr. Ayres when Cardoni was found?"

Thorpe's thin face twitched as he looked up. "Because—that was after I—*you* tell him, sir!"

Vince hesitated. "Thorpe," he said slowly, "is a sleepwalker. He walked in his sleep at the hospital, and again tonight."

"Good Lord!" exploded McKee. "Yet you permitted him to stay at large, in my ship? He might walk over the side!"

"I'd like to talk over details of this case with you in private," Vince said.

McKee looked at him sharply again. "Very well. I suppose there would never be a fingerprint on that bucket after it's been in the water this long. Come with me, doctor. Phillips, take over, here. I want a master-at-arms on each deck—I want the ship patrolled at all times!"

Thorpe sprang up in alarm. "I can't stay here, sir!" he cried.

"Turn into a bunk in the isolation ward," Vince ordered. "And shut the door."

In Captain McKee's cabin, he went over the sailor's somnambulism in detail, while the four-stripe medical officer's face grew grave.

"If he's locked up," Vince said, "I'm afraid some of my chances of getting at the bottom of this mess will be locked up with him. I'd like to keep him under observation a little longer. There was blood on that club he carried. Now he sleepwalks, and his roommate is killed!"

McKee frowned at him. "Well, it's possible. A man could commit murders in his sleep—perhaps it isn't exactly sleep, but more of a self-hypnosis. And—" he paused, and shook his head. "No, Ayres, I'm afraid you're off on the wrong track. I can't imagine any man in such a state being so damned clever as to commit any murder in the manner in which Cardoni was killed. You've got to look for somebody else!"

Vince Ayres drew a deep breath. "And find him, too," he said. "Find him quick—before he strikes again."

Excerpt from Admiral Wetherbee's log:

U.S.S. CONSOLATION, 12 January.
At sea. Anchored as before.
0600 Reveille. Begins cloudy and cold. Wind NNE by N, Force Seven.
0610 Broke out shaving gear, made all preparations for holding field day on whiskers.

0612 Hot water alongside. Clean shave, port and starboard. Cut face slightly just abaft starboard eyebrow.
Expect transfer to wheelchair this date. Must study
log of *Starfish.*

Why did THORPE, John, Sea. 2c, U. S. N., flinch
before glass he knocked from table struck his foot? Do
reflexes work for somnambulist the same as for person who is fully awake? Doubt it. Must ask medical
authority.

Understand marlin hitch was thrown about neck
of CARDONI, John Joseph, M.M. 2c, U. S. N., latest
murder victim. Clove hitch or studding-sail halliard
bend would have been more seamanlike. What kind of
knot was tied on bucket bail? Must find out.

Will question divers from *Algonquin* as soon as
they are sufficiently recovered to be up and about.

Must obtain diagram of compartments, induction
system, etc. of *Starfish.*

Believe murderer will attempt to strike at least
once more. He must be trapped then, or he may never
be found out. . . .

0700 Made all preparations for provisioning.

0702 Breakfast.

12
JOB FOR AN IRON MAN

Mike Way had a last cup of coffee in the chill morning and smoked a final cigarette while the "bears" dressed him for his dive. He felt a sense of elation, of victory over the most difficult portion of his task—they had consented to let him go down. The doctor in the *Algonquin* would never know how the big chief torpedoman had to set his teeth against the pain in his taped ribs while the doctor's fingers explored that area.

"That hurt?" the doctor had inquired. "Any tenderness there?"

Mike Way lied. "No, sir. I feel fine, sir."

A man had to lie. For his shipmates. Those twenty-five men in the *Starfish*, forty fathoms down under this gray, heaving sea. . . .

He didn't know that the doctor was echoing Vince Ayres' words of the night before. He only heard the doctor tell the *Algonquin's* skipper, "Well, if a man can swim a quarter of a mile, I guess he can dive!"

The doctor put away his stethoscope, and the skipper grunted; the skipper's eyes were bright with an admiration that belied his words.

"Captain McKee's being easy with you, chief. He could have run you up for jumping ship—leaving your post. He signaled that if you were in shape to dive, let you dive. And, by God, I'm praying for you!"

"Thank you, sir," Mike Way had said.

He had on a couple of suits of woolen underwear and three pairs of socks. He tossed his cigarette over the side where the gray water sucked greedily at the *Algonquin's* rust-stained scuppers, and took his time getting into the lead-weighted boots and the rubberized diving suit. He sat on a tool box, and the bears put the heavy breastplate over his wide shoulders.

89

"You want to watch your step, chief," one of them said as they adjusted the plate to receive his helmet. "That descending line puts you aft on the *Starfish*. Near the after rescue hatch. You got to work your way forward. You got to watch your lines. Understand?"

Mike Way understood, now. He knew the topside of that pigboat as he knew the inside of his hand. But he also fully understood the thick-headedness, the mental lethargy bordering on coma, that came so swiftly over a man under the pressure of two hundred and forty odd feet—

"Remember that, chief. You got to go forward, and keep your lines clear!"

The helmet went over Mike Way's head. He looked like a Cyclops, now. He looked like a strange creature from Mars. They screwed his helmet into place, leaving the face port open, and they buckled the forty-pound belt around his waist, connecting it with shoulder braces and the crotch strap.

"Test your telephone!"

Mike Way said, "One! Two! Three! Four!"

"Okay!" his talker reported from the other end of the line. Mike twisted the control valve on his left chest, and heard the compressed air spurt into his suit. The helpers looped his life, air and telephone lines down his back, under his arms, and up across his chest, where they were secured. His helmet port was closed and dogged down to airtight integrity with a wrench.

Somebody tapped twice on the copper helmet. Mike Way rose under weight that would have nailed a less powerful man to the deck, and was guided to the steel grating of the diving platform. He gripped the bails with his mittened hands, and waited.

"Hoist away!"

A winch puffed on the *Algonquin's* boat deck. The diving stage lifted a few feet, and the boom was swung outboard past the rail. It started down.

The gray sea came rolling. Mike Way could not look down, but out there on a level with his eyes he saw the swells lift and surge. The wind skimmed spray from their crests. A seagull rode buoyantly up a steepening slant and over; it was lost, now, behind the foam-dappled lip of the wave.

There were tons of water in each of those swells, changing the pressure that would push against Mike Way's rubberized diving suit—changing it constantly.

He felt the jar as water struck the diving stage platform. It receded, but it came again, and this time it lapped with a cold, greedy tongue at his legs.

Water came up to his face port, and swished across it. The stage stopped its descent. Mike Way spoke into his telephone:

"Take me to the descending line!"

They lifted him from the platform and carefully moved him along the lee of the tug. He wrapped his left arm around the line, and began going down.

Around him was a weird green translucence that darkened gradually. The light faded with each deepening roll of the sea. He could feel the breast plate slam against his chest every time a swell passed above; he had to valve air quickly into his suit to meet this increased pressure, and he had to be careful not to over-inflate the suit and create a positive buoyancy that would shoot him out of the water. The drag of his forty-pound belt and shoes that weighed almost half that apiece pulled him down to the accompanying roar of the compressed air in his helmet. . . .

Topside on the *Algonquin*, where the nine-ton rescue chamber waited on Mike Way's success or failure, the skipper turned from the rail with an oath that was more like a prayer.

"Signalman!" he called. "Message for Captain McKee, in the *Consolation*. Iron Man Mike Way dived at 0741."

In the isolation ward of the *Consolation*, Vince Ayres was preparing to resume the inquiry into the murder that had taken place on land, and to launch a new investigation into the one that had been committed on the high sea. He had the word passed for his party to lay below to the ward, and he waited there with Evelyn Brill.

She had not been told of Cardoni's death until morning. Consequently, she had slept despite the worry over her father's arrest, and Vince had never seen her more beautiful. He wanted to tell her this and other things, but it was neither the time nor place. And so he cursed himself for having wasted a dozen opportunities ashore, before murder followed on tragedy, and said, instead:

"I ought to hear from Simmons—the Intelligence man today. If he can find out anything important ashore, we may get somewhere. We might be able to establish a motive."

"Some murders," Evelyn said hesitantly, "are committed without motives. And aren't they usually this type—brutal, and still apparently cleverly planned? A man with a motive is apt to let it drive him. He'll kill at the first opportunity. He'll take chances."

"I'm not so sure both of these murders weren't committed at the first opportunity," Vince said. "What you say is quite true. But murder without motive means insanity—in one of its many forms. And the answer to that would be Thorpe."

"I didn't want to think he was guilty," the girl said. "But after what happened last night—I don't know."

Vince lighted a cigarette. Murphy, the redheaded corpsman from Sick Officers' Quarters, came in and waited respectfully across the room. Jacobs joined him, and then the mouselike Miss Wilkins. Vince looked at his watch impatiently.

"Thorpe may not realize how lucky he is that civil police aren't trying to find this murderer, and that newspapers aren't screaming that the fiend is still at large!" he told Evelyn in a low tone. "Because, after last night, there's enough circumstantial evidence to hang the boy a dozen times over. But I'm still reluctant to believe he's the one we want."

Kowalski entered soberly. It was easy to see a difference in the attitude of the enlisted men. One of them—Kowalski's shipmate—had been killed last night.

Then Martin West puffed in, his pudgy face still gray with anxiety and his eyes red from sleeplessness. Barbara West followed, with Victor Melhorne and Foster Bedell. Vince Ayres handed Evelyn a typewritten list—the muster roll he had used when the party boarded the *Consolation*.

"Will you please check the names, Miss Brill?" he said in a business-like manner. "Good morning, everybody."

Barbara West smiled sweetly and nodded. She was wearing a knitted sports costume of blue, and there was that warmth in

Melhorne's pale, chill eyes when he looked at her. But Vince Ayres had the sudden feeling of being in the place of a judge when a show-girl climbs to the stand and turns on all her charm. . . .

"John Thorpe isn't here, yet," Evelyn reported.

She handed the list of names back to Vince. He said, "Murphy, run out and have the word passed for Thorpe. See the master-at-arms and have him find him."

"Aye, aye, sir," the redheaded corpsman responded.

Three names were already crossed off the list. Lieutenant Ever-ett Brill—arrested and confined in his room. Mike Way—transferred. Vince smiled inwardly at the notation opposite the chief's name. And John Joseph Cardoni—murdered.

And now Martin West came forward importantly.

"Doctor," he said, "my salvage ship—the *Westsal*—is anchored over yonder, as you know."

"I know," Vince said quietly. "You want Mr. Melhorne and Mr. Bedell to be permitted to go aboard her."

"Yes—that's it." West looked surprised, as if he had expected opposition.

"I'm in favor of anything that will help rescue those men in the *Starfish*," Vince went on. He looked at his watch. "There will be a boat shoving off for the *Algonquin* in twenty minutes. I'm sure the officer of the deck will order the cox'n to take Mr. Melhorne and Mr. Bedell to the *Westsal* on that same trip."

Bedell came up, smiling warmly. "Thanks, doctor!" he said. "If you want to hold a night session when we return—"

Vince nodded. "We can decide that later. Thanks for your willing-ness to co-operate." Melhorne was talking to Barbara West, over by the door. She said, "Please be careful, Vic!" and Vince Ayres looked past them and saw Murphy coming back.

The belted master-at-arms was with the corpsman. He said, "Dr. Ayres, Thorpe is missing!"

Vince saw a smile twist off Barbara West's face. Kowalski gasped: "*Missing?*" and looked around him queerly, like a man who suddenly finds himself utterly alone. "Jeez!" he said. "Somebody gave him the deep six! And I'm the only one left—I'm the only one the murderer can get at, now!"

Vince heard the wordless little cry in Evelyn's throat. He said slowly: "But Thorpe slept here, last night. In this ward. He was told to lock the door . . ."

"We found his pajamas and his white hat here, sir," the master-at-arms explained. "He wasn't at quarters to answer muster. And then the Admiral—Admiral Wetherbee—had a search started. I guess the Admiral thinks it was suicide, sir, from what he said."

Vince watched the reaction run over these faces. Victor Melhorne snorted in disgust when the Admiral was mentioned. Miss Wilkins blanched, and Murphy said: "I thought that guy was nuts! Any guy who walks in his sleep must be nuts!"

Martin West seemed to have recovered a great deal of his confidence and his nerve. He said, "Doctor, if you think this solves the murders, let's have an end to this business! I should be on the *Westsal* myself, helping save those men. There's no earthly reason why either my daughter or I should have to remain on this ship!"

"Except," Vince said, "that nothing is solved."

"But if Thorpe drowned himself," Barbara West put in, "that was a confession of guilt!"

Vince had no chance to reply. Victor Melhorne's thin voice snapped: "This whole affair, Dr. Ayres, has been bungled! I'm a civilian, and criticism of the investigation may not be within my province. I'm not affected one way or the other by what an old man like the Admiral—in his second childhood—thinks. But the fact remains that failure to arrest Thorpe was gross negligence!"

"Vic!" Barbara West said pleadingly. "Don't make a scene!"

"Go on, Mr. Melhorne," Vince said grimly. He began to see why Barbara West was attracted to this man. He could be, after all, a masterful sort.

"I intend to!" the pale-eyed man declared stiffly. "Furthermore, if a more responsible hearing is convened later, I'll make it my duty to say the same thing. You had excellent reasons for locking Thorpe in the brig. If you believed he was a somnambulist, he should have been put there for his own protection. If he was the murderer—and every shred of evidence pointed to him—he should have been locked up for our protection!"

Vince went back a way to ask a question. "You consider the Admiral's opinions worthless, then?"

"I do!" Melhorne said coldly. "If you want me to be frank, I'd say you're a fool for paying any attention to him and his log!"

"Mr. Melhorne," Vince said, "it may be unfortunate that you aren't in charge of this inquiry. It happens that I am conducting it, and that I believe if we ever do solve the mystery, it will be largely because that log of Admiral Wetherbee's holds the key!" He glanced at his watch. "You have a boat to catch. And I will have questions to ask you later."

Melhorne started to reply heatedly, but Foster Bedell took his arm. "No use getting all steamed up, Vic," he said, and ran his palm over his chin in the way he had. "The doctor's doing the best he can. Sorry, Dr. Ayres!"

They went out. Vince said, humbly, "There may be quite a lot of truth in Mr. Melhorne's criticism. But we'll carry on. Mr. West, I'd like to ask you a few questions, if you'll step into the office."

Aft in his room, Admiral Wetherbee's shaggy brows frowned over another logbook—the one a yeoman had handed to Mike Way as the big torpedoman climbed out of the escape hatch on the *Starfish*. Two husky hospital corpsman came with a wheelchair and the information that they had been detailed to lift the Admiral into it, but he roared them away—and added, in a softer tone as they fled to the door, that he'd make the transfer later. For a long time afterward, he studied the pages of the book that had been closed so soon after its beginning.

After that, the gaunt old man lay back on his pillows and hungrily watched the sea and sky alternate in the circle of his porthole. Finally he took his own log from the bedside locker, and began to write in his small, precise hand:

0940 Commenced swinging to flood tide, stern to starboard.

1012 Receipted for log of U. S. S. STARFISH, began perusal of same.

1030 Informed instructions carried out concerning THORPE, John, Sea 2c, U. S. N.

Log of *STARFISH* trials reveals remarkable adherence to schedules drawn up by her commanding officer two weeks prior to execution of test runs. Dives scheduled thus, fourteen days in advance, performed *on the minute.* This is significant. Everybody aboard knew far ahead of time that submarine would make full crash dive at 1530 on 9 January . . .

13
UNDER PRESSURE

The green of the water turned murky blue. Mike Way could feel the pressure, now, as he slid down the descending line. He had to swallow continually to crack his ears open; the air roared in his helmet, and the talker on the *Algonquin's* deck was keeping up a running fire of conversation.

"How you doing now, chief? Feel all right?"

"Okay," Mike grunted.

"You'd better shake it up. That civilian tug over yonder is going to send a diver down if we don't make it this time. You're down two hundred. See anything?"

"I can see maybe thirty feet," Mike Way said. He gave himself more air. The pressure was becoming a part of him—it was in his tissues, in the blood and bone. It had to be equal, in his suit and in his body, to the pressure of the sea against that inflated diving rig. And at forty fathoms, the pressure of the sea was nearly a hundred and ten pounds to the square inch. . . .

Mike Way didn't want to think about this. He had to keep his mind as clear as was possible to do the job he had come down to do. He knew that the talker on deck expected him to report every move he made—when a man began losing consciousness from the pressure, his words became thick and disconnected. But he knew, too, that a hundred and ten pounds pressure is a lot; that the normal atmospheric pressure through which we walk on the surface amounts only to about thirteen pounds to the square inch.

He valved in more air, and gripped the descending line more tightly. Must be near the bottom, now. If a man landed on the whaleback of that submarine and then slipped suddenly to the ocean floor, a fatal "squeeze" would result—the pressure would change too rapidly.

He leaned forward, trying to look down. A shadowy bulk rose out of nothingness and straggled into the murk. Mike Way's voice lifted, flat and distorted under the pressure, into his telephone:

"I see her! I see the *Starfish!*"

His weighted shoes struck the wooden deck grating. He knew that twenty-five men in the torpedo room, up forward, would be hearing that welcome thump. Lieutenant James, the executive officer. Stevens, the radioman who'd been doing most of the hull-tapping. And Salty Adams, the tough and tattooed first class torpedoman—one of Mike Way's own gang.

The trouble was, he told himself, that Salty and the rest had heard divers on deck before. Several of them, since that downhaul cable carried away after the first trip of the rescue bell. They had heard divers on deck, and, after awhile—when the pressure got a man—they didn't hear him any more. He was hoisted to safety, while those in the submarine tried to crack jokes and tell themselves the next man would be able to secure that cable. . . .

"I'm on the submarine!" Mike Way reported. "Send down that cable. Damn you guys, why didn't you keep that descending line forward, where the first diver came down—when *I* was inside this pigboat?"

"Downhaul cable starting down!" the talker answered. "You be careful, chief. Don't slip over the side, now. Well, I'll tell you how it was. After that cable carried away, it came up a blow, see? We dragged our anchor. So we had to put down a grapnel, and—you okay, chief?"

"I'm okay," Mike said, but he could feel the pressure numbing his brain. "You shoot me that line . . . I'm okay."

"It's coming. Well, we had to drag the grapnel until we found her again. This time, we caught her aft."

Seconds later, Mike understood. He said, "That's a hell of a note . . . don't you drag the anchor now, sailor! Not with me down here."

The downhaul cable, shackled to the descending line, slid against his hands. He could understand why those other men had had trouble. This cable had to be unshackled and moved forward. And with every lurch of the *Algonquin* over a swell, the cable had a tendency to fly out of a man's hands.

"Ease off on the cable!" Mike said. "Give me some slack!"

He felt for his sheath knife, and cut the bit of line that shackled the cable to the descending line. He felt the pull of a swell two hundred and forty feet up, but he clung grimly to the cable and risked being jerked from the submarine's deck. Slack came, and he began walking.

"I'm going forward. I'm going past the conning tower. On the starboard side."

They could hear him; Mr. James, and Stevens and Salty; and the others. Shipmates. They could hear his weighted shoes coming nearer. . . .

"I'm going past the conning tower," he repeated, and then the cable caught on something.

"You said that," the talker shot back at him. "Where are you now?"

Mike Way pulled the cable free, and stared up at a dim projection on the conning tower. It looked like a thin, curved blade.

"That doesn't belong there," he said. "That's wrong . . . ought to tell the skipper . . . tell Dr. Ayres . . ."

"Hey—the pressure getting you?" demanded the man on deck. "Are you okay?"

"Sure!" Mike Way pulled himself back to the task at hand. "Sure, I'm all right. I'm nearly to the escape hatch . . . I'm on the escape hatch, now. I'm getting ready to shackle the cable to the hatch bail . . ."

This was the job at hand. Fix it so the rescue chamber could come down and take out those twenty-five men. Three trips, and they'd all be safe. The pressure bit into a man's blood and bone; it pounded into his ears and squeezed his brain. But he could beat it. He could win out—

"No bubble between my ears!" Mike Way growled. A man got a bubble between his ears, he was no good. Not for Navy diving.

"What's that?" the talker asked. "Chief, what are you doing?"

"I'm securing this damned downhaul cable," Mike said thickly. "I've got it secured . . . I'm walking over to the starboard rail. I'm at the rail, now . . . and you can hoist me . . . you can hoist me . . ."

Faintly, far away, he heard something in the telephone, above the roar of the compressed air and the flutter of the exhaust valve at the back of his helmet. He felt his lines grow taut, and he was being lifted from the submarine's deck.

Mike Way couldn't know that what he had heard was a cheer that burst from the throat of every man aboard the *Algonquin*.

He was pulled up to the hundred foot depth, and the diving stage had been lowered that far. He climbed on it and began a weird series of calisthenics down under the sea—began exercising in an effort to help his blood throw off its excess of nitrogen.

It would be nearly an hour before he was on the *Algonquin's* deck, allowing for proper underwater decompression, and he'd have to spend a couple of hours in the recompression chamber aboard the salvage tug in order to escape the bends.

For the first time, he became conscious of pain in those injured ribs. But he was in a hurry to get top-side—to get word to Dr. Vince Ayres. Mike Way thought he had discovered something important on the *Starfish*. . . .

At the moment, Vince was learning the curious and somewhat alarming reason for Martin West's regained self-importance and assurance. He had been questioning the shipbuilder about the contracts for construction of a score of Navy submarines. . . .

"Do you still fear, Mr. West, that your chief competitor—Pacific Maritime—may win those contracts from you?"

West looked up quickly. "I'm worried about that all right, but the rescue of those men comes first, of course. And I must admit I'm not as worried about the contract as I was, Dr. Ayres."

"Why?"

"I'm almost positive that what happened to the *Starfish* was not due to any structural fault. I think when she is raised, I'll be borne out in that confidence."

"I see," Vince nodded. There was an implication here that went beyond West's words. "Where do you think the blame lay?"

"Why, in the human factor. Man failure."

Vince looked sidewise at Evelyn Brill. She was taking notes on this interview, as she had on the others.

"Will you please explain that statement?" Vince asked.

Martin West looked at the girl, and hesitated. He said, "Could I talk to you alone?"

"Miss Brill is taking a stenographic record," Vince said. "I'd like her to note everything that is said."

"But this—this might embarrass her, doctor. I don't want to hurt her feelings—"

Evelyn Brill raised her gray eyes. They were impersonal and cool, now. She said, "Please go on, Mr. West."

"I think," the shipbuilder began slowly, "that the captain—Lieutenant Brill—erred in some way. There are so many responsibilities resting on the captain of a submarine; it would be only human to forget something. Such as failing to ascertain if all the induction valves are closed before giving the order for a full crash dive. You—you see what I mean?"

"Yes," Vince said. "What makes you think this?"

West hesitated again. "This is more serious!" he blurted. "I'm not accusing Lieutenant Brill—please understand that. I'm not accusing him of the murder—the murders. But after studying the case, I have come to the conclusion that he alone had sufficient motive. His negligence had to be covered up. McQuaid intended to testify that Brill was intoxicated—McQuaid was killed. Cardoni might possibly have known what went on back aft—and Cardoni was killed. That left Thorpe, who also might have remembered something that would incriminate the skipper, after his shock wore off—and Thorpe has disappeared! I'm—I'm sorry, Miss Brill."

Vince watched the flush creeping into Evelyn's cheeks. She was more lovely than ever when she was angry, he decided. He shook his head when West had finished.

"The assumption that Brill might have killed McQuaid perhaps could be called as logical as any theory we've so far developed," he said. "The Commandant may have acted on the same suspicion when he ordered Brill arrested. But that arrest causes the entire theory to collapse when it is applied to Cardoni's murder. If the same man killed both—and you'll agree that's likely—Lieutenant Brill must be left out. He's been locked up since yesterday morning, as you know."

"I was coming to that," West said. He leaned forward, his gray face intense. "Dr. Ayres, I was on deck last night—with Bedell and Melhorne. We watched the lights of the *Westsal* as she steamed up."

"I know," Vince nodded. "I saw you there."

"Well, when we went below again, we—we saw Brill in the passageway. *Near Cardoni's room!* He could have been leaving it. He certainly wasn't locked up just then. Bedell and Melhorne will bear me out in this statement!"

Evelyn's pen faltered. Vince saw that her cheeks had gone white, and her hand was trembling. He said: "You're sure? Was anybody with him—a guard?"

"It was Lieutenant Brill. And he was alone!"

Vince rose heavily. "Thank you, Mr. West," he said. "I'll question Lieutenant Brill about the matter. Thank you for your co-operation."

It was nearly time for the noon meal. Vince dismissed the others, and thought he saw triumph in Barbara West's dark eyes when she looked at Evelyn. He sat on a corner of the nurse's desk and thoughtfully lighted a cigarette.

Evelyn said in a strained voice, "Well—it gets worse instead of better! Poor Dad! Vince, if he is tried for this thing, it won't make much difference how the trial comes out—it'll kill him, one way or the other! His career will be ruined, and that's his life."

"Don't give up the ship, matey!" Vince smiled. He reached out to squeeze her hand. "I know this looks bad, but it probably will be proved purely coincidental. I think Mr. West—encouraged by his daughter—is indulging in a lot of wishful thinking along deductive lines!"

"How do you mean?"

"Well, I may be guilty of wishful thinking, too," Vince confessed. "But the change in West's attitude, and that of his daughter, might mean that a load has been taken off their minds by the fact that they've been able to figure out that your father is the guilty person. In other words, perhaps they've been hoping two things: West, that there wasn't anything wrong with the submarine he'd built, and Barbara—that Victor Melhorne didn't have anything to do with McQuaid's murder. Ever since she saw that man on the balcony, she's been secretly afraid that Melhorne was the killer. Oh, this is all speculation, Evelyn, but what else have we got right now?"

The girl sighed. "It doesn't help Dad, I'm afraid. Unless he can explain. He has one more thing to explain, now!"

A messenger from the radio room entered the ward. Vince sprang up from the desk to sign for the yellow communications sheet. He read it swiftly, and then held it out so that Evelyn could see.

RADIO NINETEENTH NAVAL TWELFTH 1139 BT
LIEUT. VINCENT AYRES MC USN USS CONSOLA-
TION BT
NIGHT WATCHMAN MCCARTHY VERY MUCH
AFRAID OF LOSING JOB BUT FINALLY RELUC-
TANTLY ADMITTED HE STRUCK THORPE NIGHT
OF MURDER WITH BILLIARD CUE AFTER WREST-
ING IT FROM THORPE'S HANDS. EXPECT TO BE
ABLE TO TRANSMIT OTHER INFO YOU REQUEST-
ED LATER TODAY BT
SIMMONS
TOD 1146

"There," said Vince, "goes part of the case we had built up against young Thorpe—in spite of Melhorne's certainty that the boy is the killer. It was Thorpe's blood on the club. Of course, it was raining. There could have been blood on the billiard cue already."

"Vince," said Evelyn, "you'd make a better defense attorney than a prosecutor, I'm afraid!"

He smiled. "I guess so. I've officiated at two courts martial—both times for the defense. Well, I'm glad to learn this, even if it doesn't help us any right now."

"It doesn't help John Thorpe, either," she reminded him. "It might have—if the report had come last night. Before he fell or was pushed over the side. . . ."

Vince Ayres smiled strangely. "Remember what I said, matey! Don't give up the ship. And don't believe Thorpe is dead until they've found his body!"

14

UP FROM THE BOTTOM

The *Algonquin's* rescue bell made its first descent before noon. Something of the joyful excitement that reigned aboard the rescue ship was transmitted to the *Consolation*, but there was tenseness, too. The sea was fully as rough as it had been on that earlier trip, the day the downhaul cable had parted.

Vince Ayres knew it would be almost useless to attempt to question anybody while the anxiety was upon them, and so he recessed the investigation for the time being. Evelyn Brill went to Admiral Wetherbee's room.

She found him reading Mahan's *The Interest of America in Sea Power, Present and Future*. He put the book aside with a twinkle in his sea-blue eyes, and smiled at her.

"Feeling better about things?"

She shook her head. "Worse. Mr. West just told us that he saw Dad near Cardoni's room last night—about the time the—the murder was committed. That will be brought out if Dad comes to trial. And just when I thought the Cardoni murder at least cleared Dad of any suspicion in the other one—because I thought he was locked up in his room!"

Admiral Wetherbee reached for his logbook. "Let me read you an entry I made last night," he said. "'2130'—that's half-past nine, you know—'2130 Received Lieut. EVERETT BRILL, USN, commanding USS STARFISH, for questioning concerning loss of his ship. 2145 Completed examination of Lieut. BRILL.'"

Evelyn said, "He was here, then! But that doesn't clear him. He was here only fifteen minutes. And the sentry must have brought him—where was the sentry when West saw him? West says he was alone."

"I wouldn't want to get that sailor on the report," the Admiral said thoughtfully. "The fact is, I sent him to see if he could find me a turkey leg. Before he came back with it, your father had finished telling me all he knew about the *Starfish*, and had gone on back to his room. Irregular, yes—but I'll assume responsibility for it if anything is said. After all, a strict guard is hardly necessary in his case. Just a matter of form."

He was minimizing the irregularity, Evelyn knew, for her benefit. There was something under the surface, here; she felt that the shaggy-browed old man knew something he wasn't telling her just now.

"I'm discouraged at our failure to find one tangible clue!" she said. "We could never prove, now, that John Thorpe did the killings—even if he really were the murderer. Unless they are definitely solved, there'll be a cloud that will hang over Dad the rest of his time in the Service. You know that. Oh, I ought to be happy that rescue seems so near for the rest of his men! But I suppose I'm selfish. Those twenty-five men can't help us any."

Admiral Wetherbee frowned. "Don't be too sure about that," he rumbled. "I'll tell you—I want you to do something for me!" He looked around cautiously, as if afraid of an eavesdropper. "I want you to carry on a little investigation. Those *Starfish* survivors don't know you. They'll be turned in as patients, and it should be easy for you to stand a few ward watches. Ask them some questions. Ask about the feuds that apparently existed in the ship. And about that mysterious smell McQuaid kept raving about."

"I'll do what you suggest," the girl said disconsolately. "But I don't imagine it will accomplish much—they'll probably tell me what we've already heard. They'll say Lieutenant McQuaid thought he smelled liquor on Dad's breath and doubted that he was in shape to command."

"Maybe they will," the Admiral returned. "But it could have been a dozen other things, Evelyn. Smells are important in a submarine. The batteries—gas from the batteries! Water came in with a rush, apparently, but perhaps there was water from below, earlier, and not immediately noticed. It might have got in the batteries and caused a chlorine smell, which McQuaid would have recognized at once. Hell's bells! Why didn't I think of that before? Chlorine gas gets a man pretty fast. Water in the batteries—the electrical system short-circuiting—an explosion would be certain to follow . . ."

He reached for the logbook again, and made an entry. He skimmed back a couple of pages, and asked abruptly: "What do you think of Victor Melhorne?"

"I don't like him," Evelyn said. "But he appears to be an honest sort—aboveboard and frank. He accused Vince, today, of mishandling the investigation."

"Yes, I know," the Admiral murmured. He lay back, his eyes half-closed, as if thinking deeply. He was strange, Evelyn thought, but priceless. Apparently he had sources of information so well organized that nothing escaped him. And he had the time to lie here and weigh one fact against another.

"We've been too much on the defensive, Evelyn!" he rumbled suddenly. "That's no good. In war—in the fight toward any goal—offense is the best defense. What is it Mahan said? 'The enemy must not be fended off, but smitten down . . . till down, he must be struck incessantly and remorselessly.' That's what we've got to do. Trap this murderer. Get him under our guns!"

Evelyn could not suppress a smile. She said, "That would be the proper tactics, Admiral, if we only had a faint knowledge of what he looks like—if we weren't misled by a dozen false clues that lead nowhere!"

The Admiral chuckled. "It happens," he said quietly, "that I know who the murderer is! Knowing it and proving it are two different matters. It will require a little time. . . ."

Vince Ayres came with the glad word that a motor sailer was coming alongside with the first eight men to be brought up from the *Starfish.* Evelyn hurried topside with him, and they stood near the gangway as the launch approached the big white ship. She saw the pigboat sailors, blankets wrapped around their shoulders, sitting on the thwarts; the sullen gray sea tossed the boat as if in a final resentment at having been cheated. Half the crew of the *Consolation* was here at the rail to cheer the men from the bottom, but the sight of their upturned faces, bearded and drawn and still filled now with a great and simple happiness, brought a catch to the girl's throat.

She saw Kowalski's curly head bent over the rail. He yelled down excitedly: "Hey, Salty! Salty Adams, you old son-of-a-gun!" And he made a swipe, unashamed, at a moisture in his eyes.

A redheaded man in water-soaked dungarees looked up at the *Consolation*. He was carrying a heavy three-inch cartridge case that had been partly converted into an ornate lamp stand—it was the same souvenir to which he had clung in that cold and crowded forward torpedo room. Salty Adams had lost all his clothing except the dungarees he wore, but clothes didn't count. He'd put in a lot of spare time work on this souvenir.

"What d'ye say, Skee?" he chortled. Then, in sudden realization: "Hey, what the hell are you doing here? I thought they made a speed run to the hospital with you guys!"

"They did," the square-faced Kowalski answered. "But they shanghaied us to sea again. The skipper's aboard, too, Salty. Did you see Mike Way?"

Adams grinned as he came up the gangway, scorning the assistance offered by hospital corpsmen. "Sure!" he said. "He was in the iron doctor, but I had a look at him through the port. If it hadn't been for old Iron Man, we'd still be on the bottom!"

"Has he got bends?" Kowalski asked in concern.

"Yeah—some. Not bad, they told us. Where'll I find Dr. Ayres? Mike gave me a note for him."

Vince stepped forward and took the submarine sailor's arm. Salty Adams paused for his salute to the quarterdeck; it was given in a way that made everybody know that the first class torpedoman would make another full crash dive in another submarine tomorrow, if the Navy said the word.

"I'm Ayres," Vince said. Evelyn Brill was remembering that these men from the bottom had heard nothing of the two murders, nothing of young John Thorpe's disappearance. Time had stopped, for a little while, as far as they were concerned.

Adams shifted the brass cartridge case to the crook of his left arm, and searched his pockets. "He didn't have much time to write it, sir," he said as he produced the folded paper. "He had to send it out through the air lock. I saw the pressure gauge—they had the chief under eighty pounds. But he wrote this and told 'em to tell me it was important."

"Thank you," Vince said.

The blanketed men were hustled into a ward. Vince passed the note to Evelyn. It was brief:

> *Found something that looks important but will have*
> *to dive again to make sure. Next trip of the bell I will*
> *have somebody bring up that bottle.*
> MIKE WAY, CTM

There was work to do, and Evelyn would have no chance to ask questions until later. The men were given hot drinks and were further warmed and stimulated by the application of hot water bottles and electric pads. When the rescue bell brought up the second group of eight an hour and a half later, the first men had fallen fast asleep.

The big chamber took the remaining nine out of the *Starfish* in its final trip. Lieutenant James, the small, imperturbable executive officer, was the last man to climb out of the torpedo room. When he reached the hospital ship, his first inquiry was for the man who should have had the honor of leaving the *Starfish* last—his skipper.

"He was a sick man," James said when Vince Ayres assured him that Everett Brill was well. "If he'd stayed down there, it might have killed him." He smiled, remembering the circumstances of Brill's leaving. "Did he say anything about it—about being shanghaied out of there, I mean?"

Vince nodded. "He was pretty sore about it. Said somebody hit him in the dark."

And for the first time, the doctor wondered if that blow in the darkness had missed its real purpose. Was the murderer intending to start his work down there in the submarine?

"Somebody did," James grunted. "How's McQuaid?"

"He—he didn't come back to sea," Vince evaded. It would be time enough later for Lieutenant James to learn that McQuaid had been murdered, and that Everett Brill might soon face a court martial that would be as unwelcome to him as death itself.

Working, that afternoon, Evelyn Brill kept wondering at what Admiral Wetherbee had said. *It happens that I know who the murderer is.* . . .

There was a possibility that the old sea dog had seen and heard more, on the rainy midnight when McQuaid was killed, than he had ever revealed to anybody. It might, she thought, be set down in the logbook he kept so faithfully.

You can't fool around with the decompression table, which is based on physical laws. And the bends are unpredictable: pressure undergone today may double a diver in agony the day after tomorrow if all the nitrogen has not escaped from his blood. Mike Way had been down at that forty fathom depth beyond the safe time limit; he spent an hour at various ten-foot levels ranging from the hundred-foot depth upward, and he had more than two hours in the recompression chamber aboard the *Algonquin*.

His head cleared slowly. What he had found down there on the *Starfish* seemed improbable, now, like a dream. But if it were true, many things might be at least partly explained—even murder.

"I got to dive again!" the big chief torpedoman kept telling himself. "I got to go into that after escape hatch. Before they hang the skipper for something he didn't do."

But the doctor aboard the salvage tug said no. It was with great difficulty that Mike Way convinced the medical officer that he was all right again—that he could go back to the *Consolation* and report to Vince Ayres.

15
MOTIVE FOR A WOMAN

Melhorne and Bedell returned to the hospital ship just before dark, and when Vince Ayres reconvened the murder investigation in the little isolation ward just after supper, he heard the two men and Martin West deep in a discussion of salvage methods. There was a good chance, it seemed, that the Navy would temporarily leave the problem of raising the ship to the Westco firm.

This cheered Martin West. "If they do that," he said happily, "it indicates that the government has every confidence in our design and construction. If they thought the ship had failed, they'd want to get it up for a quick and thorough examination."

Foster Bedell shook his head dubiously. "I'm not so sure about that, Mr. West," he said. "Divers can enter the flooded portion of the *Starfish*, and make a pretty fair examination of her as she lies. I mean to say that we shouldn't delay, due to any fears of our own that something *might* have gone wrong due to weakness. We've got to show a willingness to co-operate. How long will it take to get the necessary pontoons out here?"

Melhorne said, "About three days. They tow slowly."

Barbara West came in, smiling at the man to whom she was secretly engaged. Watching her, Vince Ayres wondered why the secrecy was necessary. He supposed, charitably, that publicity linked to the submarine tragedy—and, later, to the murders—would have smacked of notoriety.

He called on Bedell, first, but before they had gone into the nurse's office a hospital corpsman came with excerpts copied from

Admiral Wetherbee's log. Vince called the group to attention, and read the entries:

> 1310 Eight men rescued from U. S. S. STARFISH brought aboard pursuant to orders of Commandant Nineteenth Naval for hospitalization of all STARFISH survivors.
>
> 1320 Resumed study of STARFISH log. . . . NOTE: Identification of the murderer is possible at this point, through a mathematical process no more difficult than a navigational problem. Identity, however, must be kept secret for the time being in order to determine whether or not guilty person had accomplices.
>
> Conclude from observations that two persons who have been under scrutiny and questioning are attempting to shield each other. Could this mean one is an accomplice, or does each fear other is guilty? Must consider motives here, and reasons for this fear.
>
> CARDONI murder committed in a clever but lubberly fashion. Purpose of it was to cover up, but in killing CARDONI the murderer has provided an excellent clue: murderer would have been safer if CARDONI were still alive.
>
> 1450 Second contingent of STARFISH survivors brought aboard. Must talk to them when they are able to be questioned.
>
> 1520 Pursuant to radio orders received from commandant Nineteenth Naval District, began to prepare personal log, with final summations of case, for presentation to board of inquiry scheduled to be called ashore immediately upon return of U. S. S. CONSOLATION to port.
>
> 1530 What did WAY, MICHAEL, C. T. M. U. S. N. discover on topside of STARFISH which he considers pertinent to this investigation? WAY deserves commendation for bravery exhibited in perilous dive.
>
> MEMO TO LIEUT. AYRES: Please carry on.

There was a silence when Vince Ayres had finished reading the log entry. A dubious silence, for the most part, he saw when he noted the expressions worn by those who had heard. He folded the paper into his pocket, and polished his gold-rimmed glasses before he spoke.

"It would be a great mistake—a fatal mistake, so far as the murderer is concerned—to underestimate the importance or the accuracy of Admiral Wetherbee's log," he said quietly. "But we will proceed as he suggests. Will you come in, Mr. Bedell?"

The dark-faced man nodded and followed Evelyn into the nurse's office. He was more at ease than most of those Vince had previously questioned, but he had less to tell. He had heard nothing at the hospital on the night McQuaid was killed. Yes, he had seen Everett Brill in the passageway a few doors from Cardoni's room. . . .

"But I attached no significance to it," he said with a reassuring glance toward Evelyn. "In fact, I can't quite understand why the captain should have been placed in custody at all."

Vince toyed with a clinical thermometer, pencil-wise. "Mr. West has a different opinion," he said. "He thinks Brill is the most likely suspect because he firmly believes some negligence on the captain's part was responsible for the *Starfish* disaster. You have noticed, of course, that the two murders and Thorpe's disappearance preclude any possibility of discovering what happened in the after portion of the submarine until she is raised?"

"Why, yes," Bedell said. He pulled his dark brows together, in that intent way rubbed his chin, and hesitated. "I don't wish to appear disloyal to Mr. West, doctor. But I don't share his belief. I was in the control room most of the time preceding that full crash dive, and I'm sure the captain handled his ship quite properly. I don't think he had anything to cover up—by murder or otherwise."

"Then the loss of the ship—" Vince began.

"Who can say?" Bedell asked. He pursed his lips and resumed slowly: "Submarines are tricky. Something went wrong. Water tight integrity failed at some vital point. That's my honest belief."

Vince regarded the designer thoughtfully and with full appreciation of what Bedell was saying. If the Navy thought as Bedell did, Westco would be likely to lose the contract for construction of those remaining submarines.

"You don't think the *Starfish* struck anything—any submerged object?" the doctor asked.

"I don't think so," Bedell said. "The sea was quite rough, and there was considerable noise in the ship. But we would have felt any jar sufficient to rip the hull."

"Well," Vince pursued, "your theory eliminates one of the strongest possible murder motives. Now what do you believe *was* the motive, and who is the murderer?"

"I think there may be some truth in what Vic Melhorne said—about Thorpe," Bedell declared. "His first sleepwalking—if it really was sleepwalking—could have been purely coincidental. But when a thing happens too often, it ceases to be coincidence. I think Cardoni's murder and Thorpe's apparent suicide proved the entire case. As for a motive—" and Foster Bedell shrugged "—there doesn't appear to have been any beyond that of revenge against Lieutenant McQuaid for a fancied wrong, and a subsequently growing psychosis—something you'd understand better than I. Perhaps Cardoni teased the boy. Or, perhaps something Cardoni said led Thorpe to believe Cardoni knew too much."

After Bedell had gone, the doctor smiled at Evelyn. "There," he said, "was an unexpected champion for your father! I imagined these four civilians would stick together closer than brothers, especially since they're responsible for the building of the submarine. It's surprising that Bedell would admit the ship might have been at fault."

"It's refreshing!" Evelyn said. "At least, Mr. Bedell is honest, and I'm very grateful to him. Vince—who did the Admiral mean when he said at least two persons were trying to protect each other? Barbara West and Melhorne?"

"Of course," Vince told her. "We've seen it. Miss West stalled and then finally admitted she was on the balcony, and that she fled when she saw the man with the club. We're pretty certain that she fears that man was Melhorne. Why—I mean how she justifies this fear by way of a motive that would lead Melhorne to kill McQuaid—I don't know. But, for the same unknown reason, Melhorne may be nursing a secret fear that Barbara committed the murder. He knows, no doubt, that she was out there that night. What that mutual suspicion is based on—we must try to find out!"

He called Melhorne into the office. The pale-eyed man was cold-ly polite, and as frank as he had been earlier in the day. In his thin voice, he repeated his assertion that John Thorpe should have been arrested.

"Let's get back to the night at the hospital," Vince said abruptly. "Did you hear anybody at your window?"

Melhorne hesitated perceptibly. "Why, no, I didn't."

"Would you say you slept so soundly that a man—the murderer, Mr. Melhorne—could have come through your room from the hall?"

"I wouldn't know how soundly I slept!" Melhorne said angrily. "You'll agree that I had reason to sleep hard. I was tired."

"You wouldn't even have heard Miss West calling you from the open window?"

Melhorne sprang to his feet, flushing. "What are you getting at, doctor?"

"The fact that she has told me she was out there—and that you must have known it. She has told you, too, before now. Are you at-tempting to protect her from anything definite, Melhorne? Are you afraid she might be accused?"

The stocky man bit his lip. "I resent this line of questioning, doc-tor!" he protested. "It's absurd to hint, in the slightest degree, that Miss West could have had anything to do with either murder. You had your man, and you let him get away. You're trying to cover up, now, by—"

A scream came from the ward. Those in the nurse's office whirled, startled by the cry, and Vince Ayres saw that it had been the mouse-like Miss Wilkins who uttered it. She was pointing toward the door, her face pale and her eyes wide.

Vince ran out into the ward. All he could see was a messenger from the radio room, closing the door behind him as he brought a yellow communications sheet.

Miss Wilkins recovered speech. "Thorpe!" she cried in a strained, high-pitched voice. "He went by the door! He—he looked like a ghost!"

"Ridiculous!" Vince said. But he went quickly to the door and opened it. The passageway was deserted.

"I saw him, doctor!" the nurse insisted. "I'm not superstitious, of course. It really was Thorpe. But he was very pale, and he wore a white sheet!"

Foster Bedell smiled. "We'll all be seeing things before long, I'm afraid!"

Vince turned to the messenger. "Did you see anybody in the passageway?"

"No, sir," the round-eyed sailor said. "I didn't look behind me, but I'd have heard them, I'm sure. Will—will you sign for this radio, sir? And Way, the chief torpedoman, has been turned in at his room, Dr. Ayres, and he asked me to tell you that he'd like to see you on a matter of great importance."

Vince signed and glanced hurriedly through the message. He said, as if preoccupied by its contents, "I think that will be all for tonight. Messenger—tell the chief I'll come to his room in five minutes. Well . . . let's not start seeing ghosts, please! Good night."

Evelyn Brill remained at a signal from him, the pad of temperature charts still in her hand. She said: "I'll have to do quite a bit of typing to transcribe this record up to date! Anything of importance from ashore, Vince?"

"Important?" he repeated slowly. "Maybe. But I wouldn't think it would be important enough for murder. It's like some of the other stuff we've found—it could be a motive provided we stretch our imagination. Read it."

RADIO NINETEENTH NAVAL TWELFTH BT
LIEUT. VINCENT AYRES USS CONSOLATION BT
HAVE FOUND WITNESS TO QUARREL BETWEEN
MCQUAID AND MELHORNE AT ARMY AND NAVY
CLUB DISPUTE WAS OVER TECHNICAL ARTICLE
MCQUAID WAS PREPARING FOR MAGAZINE SUP-
POSEDLY CRITICIZING SUBMARINES OF STAR-
FISH TYPE MELHORNE DEFENDED SHIPS AND
ACCUSED MCQUAID OF QUOTE SABOTAGING
NATIONAL DEFENSE PROGRAM IF HE PUB-
LISHED ARTICLE UNQUOTE BARBARA WEST WAS
PRESENT BT
SIMMONS
TOD 2120

Evelyn drew a long breath and stared thoughtfully at the door where Barbara West had gone with the shipbuilder and the others. She 'said, "No, I'm afraid it doesn't help much, Vince. The Navy encourages its officers to write technical articles, so long as it is made plain they are expressing their own views. Naturally, Melhorne would defend the ships he's helping design and build."

"But he wouldn't be likely to kill a man who held a different opinion," Vince nodded. "Except—well, as I said before, that would be stretching the imagination quite a bit!"

"Except what?"

Vince Ayres polished his glasses before replying. "It's pretty easy to see Martin West is more worried about those contracts than he'll admit. Mike Way found something on the *Starfish*. Maybe she didn't sink accidentally—and if she did, something was very wrong. Maybe McQuaid knew that something!"

16
MURDER'S FIRST MISS

Mike Way enjoyed luxury scarcely consistent with his rating of chief torpedoman. It was a far cry from the crowded quarters of a submarine, or the almost equally-jammed space of the "guinea pullman" aboard a destroyer, to the quiet room in which the big, ugly diver had been placed aboard the *Consolation*. This had been a first-class cabin in the days before the Navy converted the ship from a passenger liner; it was above the main deck, well-lighted and well-ventilated by portholes opening on the promenade.

He grinned from his bunk as Vince Ayres entered.

The doctor said, "Hello, chief!" and looked sharply at a crimson splotch on the diver's forehead.

That was blood, oozing from broken capillaries. Pressure, finding its way out of Mike Way's rugged body. He'd been under too long at that extreme depth where the *Starfish* lay.

"Doctor," the chief said, "they told me about Cardoni. And John Thorpe. Do you think somebody pushed that kid? Or do you figure it was suicide . . . because he did the killings?"

Vince said, "I've about given up trying to figure all these angles. And I'm not even sure that Thorpe has gone over the side. Miss Wilkins swears she saw him go by the door of the isolation ward, a little while ago!"

"But, good Lord, doctor—a man can't hide out aboard ship! Not for long. They told me they looked everywhere for him—"

"Not without help, he couldn't hide out," Vince said. "I don't know. I saw an entry in the Admiral's log which might mean something, but I didn't ask any questions. It said, 'Informed instructions carried out concerning Thorpe . . .' But I came here to hear you tell me something important, not to speculate on things. How do you feel?"

"Fine—just fine, sir. I've got to dive again. They shouldn't have sent me back over here. I've got to be the first diver inside that flooded portion of the *Starfish!*"

"You look fine!" Vince said sarcastically. "How long were you down?"

"About forty-five minutes, sir."

"Or nearly three times as long as is advisable at that depth!" said the doctor. He wiped his gold-rimmed glasses and gave Mike Way one of those quiet, clear-eyed looks. "You did a great job, chief," he added softly. "Those twenty-five men probably owe you their lives."

"Oh, somebody would have got that cable secured, if I hadn't," Mike Way said modestly. He winced suddenly, and cautiously lifted one muscular arm. It was swollen around the elbow.

"You've got the bends right now!" Vince Ayres exclaimed. "You'd better jump into a tub of boiling hot water. I'll have a couple of corpsmen get it ready."

"Not now, sir," pleaded Mike Way. "This is only a slight attack—I've had 'em bad, before. Doctor . . . maybe I found something, and maybe I didn't. It's crazy—it doesn't belong. But if the murders have anything to do with the sinking of that pigboat—"

His voice was high, excited. Vince pulled his chair closer, and leaned toward the man in the bunk.

"Go on," he said. "We don't know, yet. But, after all, the men who have been put out of the way were men who escaped from the flooded compartments, and that looks significant. Go on!"

Mike Way winced again under a spasm of pain that struck somewhere in his nitrogen-saturated body. Between his teeth, he said:

"When I was working my way past the conning tower, my lines caught on something above my head. I looked up. You know those vents in the skin of the ship—the ones that take in air when she's on the surface? Well, this gadget was sticking out of one of them. It—"

Vince Ayres heard a slight scraping sound at the porthole. He said, cautiously: "Wait, chief," and turned that way. Blue steel glinted against the brass, and there was a dark shadow where the light should have fallen.

Vince yelled a warning as he leaped, spinning his chair around to crash against Mike Way's bunk. He slapped the light switch by the door. The room went dark.

Then gun flashes ripped brightly through the porthole. One—two—three shots. Vince heard the flattening drive of slugs against the bulkhead, heard them ricochet within the room. He sprang to the porthole, risking a bullet to grab at that gun, to seize the hand which held it.

But he was too late. He stood there, breathing hard, feeling helpless as the acrid smell of powder drifted through the room. All was quiet inside, but he heard shoes click swiftly on the deck. The assassin was running aft.

Vince cursed, and hit the light switch again, afraid of what he would see. He yelled, "Are you hurt, chief?" before his eyes could adjust themselves to the returned light, and he waited at the doorway for Mike's slow answer. People were coming up excitedly outside. It came to Vince that before he could reach the promenade deck, the person who had fired those shots would have had his choice of ducking into a dozen different places.

"No, sir," said Mike Way with laborious, pain-locked effort. "Wasn't hit—just—bends! They're bad—now!"

The door flew open. A pharmacist's mate burst in excitedly. Kowalski was at his heels—Kowalski's face was nearly as drab as the adhesive tape that covered that cut he'd suffered in the *Starfish*. Then came Foster Bedell, and Evelyn Brill; Martin West and Melhorne and others jammed the doorway.

Vince seized Evelyn's arm. "Take charge here!" he told her. "One of you men get a doctor. He wasn't hit, but he's got the bends—got them bad!"

He saw her nod with quick understanding, and he went on amidships where a door opened on the promenade deck, knowing heavily that his search would be futile. There was nobody on the dimly-lighted deck; there was nothing in sight to give a clue to the identity of the person who had feared what Mike Way was going to say.

Vince came to the open porthole through which the gun had been thrust. He heard Foster Bedell's vice inside, saying: "Didn't you see him, Way—did you get a glimpse of his face?" And instead of answering, Mike Way wrenched a groan between his set teeth, and the sound almost became a scream.

Vince Ayres knew what the bends could do. If they were bad enough, the big diver might lose consciousness. The bends could twist a man's stomach in a knot and set fire to it. Nothing that could happen to a man quite compared with this agony. . . .

He swore again, and turned away. But he remembered something. The waterway that ran like a gutter along the deck beneath the rail to drain off high-lashing seas. He struck a match and cupped the flame in his palm against the wind, and he found what he was looking for—an empty shell.

There was only one. Thirty-two caliber automatic. At least he knew what kind of gun to look for. A gun the Navy didn't use, he told himself. A gun small enough for a woman to carry. . . .

They were carrying Mike Way out in Stoke's basket litter when Vince came back to the passageway, and Vince knew that the attack was too severe to be remedied by immersion in bath water that was nearly scalding. He overtook the doctor Evelyn had summoned—a sturdy young junior grade attached to the *Consolation's* so far skeleton staff.

"He's got to be put under compression again, Dr. Ayres," the stripe-and-a-half officer reported. "I gave him an injection, and called away the officers' motor boat to get him over to the *Algonquin* quickly. We have no recompression tank aboard yet."

Vince nodded, and heard the sputter of the motor boat as it came around the lee of the ship to make the accommodation ladder. The stretcher bearers went down to the main deck, and Mike Way's cries drifted up through the ship.

Evelyn Brill's gray eyes were wet. She said, "It takes something to make that man cry out! I know. He was my patient once, and he had bends bad enough, then. This time they must be worse. Thank God the murderer missed him! After all he's done for his shipmates . . . and for Dad!"

"He'll be all right, Evelyn," Vince said gently. "They don't call him Iron Man for nothing—he was under pressure enough to kill the average man! They'll feed him oxygen in the tank, and he'll be all right by morning. Let's look in his room."

They found white lead chipped from the bulkhead in two places; inches from where Mike Way's head had been. The third shot had struck the mattress itself.

Captain McKee loomed in the doorway, tall and commanding, and now very grim. He listened silently to Vince's report, and examined the shell Vince had found in the waterway.

"I'll have this ship searched from double bottoms to crow's nest!" he said. "But it would have been an easy matter for the man who fired those shots to throw the gun over the side. See here, Dr. Ayres, you're in charge of this investigation and your party came aboard somewhat as an independent command! I was told to give you free rein and to co-operate with you as much as possible. But damn it all, something's got to be done—at once!"

Vince stiffened. "Captain, I think we're beginning to get somewhere. I—"

"Get somewhere?" McKee echoed. "With a murder a day and a few assorted attempts on the side? I want action! I'll expect solution of these crimes quickly, or I shall have to take steps of my own to protect the security of this ship and the lives of everybody in her!"

"May I ask what you'd do?" Vince inquired quietly.

"Lock every member of your party in the brig and in their rooms— separately and individually!" McKee snapped. "It's apparent that when Lieutenant Brill was arrested on orders from shore, the wrong man was locked up. It's apparent, now, that young Thorpe was the innocent victim of his own affliction—sleepwalking. The murderer, doctor, is still at large!"

He paused, and glared at Vince. "Do I make myself clear, sir?"

"Perfectly, captain!" Vince said. "I understand your feelings. But such a procedure would hinder two things, sir. First, the investigation itself. We haven't had much to go on. I've depended a lot on the psychological effect of calling these people together and watching them—studying their reactions. I may say that we've uncovered a couple of good leads in that manner."

"Go on," McKee said grimly.

"Then there are the salvage operations, sir. Melhorne and Bedell have active charge of the work done by the civilian crew on the *Westsal*. They went aboard her today and are scheduled to do the same tomorrow. I question whether it's advisable to do anything that might delay or jeopardize the raising of the *Starfish*, captain. We may not solve these crimes until we learn what actually happened aboard that submarine."

Captain McKee looked up significantly. "You mean . . . ?"

"I mean that there is a possibility that these murders were an attempt to cover up the murders of twenty-two other men, sir!"

The gray-haired four-striper clicked his jaw shut. "Very well, Dr. Ayres!" he said briskly. "I'll give you twenty-four hours. If there's been no action by that time, I shall report to the commandant of Nineteenth Naval and ask that I be given full charge!"

"Aye, aye, sir," Vince said, and watched Captain McKee stalk away looking far more military than any other medical officer he had ever known.

Then he turned to Evelyn with a rueful look. "I guess we've failed, all right," he said. "It's funny. Suspicions point to a half dozen people; actual evidence doesn't point to anybody! And I rack my brains all day and study and watch these people—and the only real progress seems to come from that old sea dog back yonder, who does nothing but lie there and think things out! Did you give him that radio from Simmons, Evelyn?"

"Yes. He had Lieutenant James—the executive officer from the *Starfish*—in his room. They were talking about the design of the submarine."

Vince said, "Well, he insists—in his log, anyway—that he knows who the murderer is. All right. He'd better tell us who it is, before another murder is committed! Let's go talk to him."

17
IRON MAN, IRON DOCTOR

Mike Way came back to dim consciousness in the *Algonquin's* recompression tank, shouting and fighting against the doctor and the pharmacist's mate who were massaging his arms and legs. But the struggle was brief, and the big man pulled himself to a sitting position.

"What time is it?" he demanded. "How long have I been in here?"

The doctor smiled. "Less than an hour, chief. But you're going to be here a lot longer. You're going to spend the night in here, just to make sure!"

Mike lay back down. "That's all right, sir—to stay all night. But in the morning, I got to dive!"

He glanced at the pressure gauge. Forty-five pounds approximately a hundred feet. And the doctor and pharmacist's mate grinned at each other.

"What are you trying to do, chief?" the corpsman asked humorously. "Make a rate?"

"I got to dive!" Mike said stubbornly.

"We'll talk about that later," the doctor promised. "I'd hate to see you cripple yourself for life."

"I can take it," Mike declared. "Just once more, doctor. After I come up that time, I'll spend a week in this tank if necessary. But a lot depends on that dive, now."

"I sent you back to the *Consolation* too soon, as it was," said the doctor. "The bends are tricky. It's hard to tell when the danger is past."

Mike Way frowned. He was just remembering that somebody—the murderer—had taken three shots at him as he lay in his bunk on the *Consolation*. He remembered that a sudden spasm of the bends had doubled him up an instant before that gun began popping in the porthole. It was funny, but the bends probably had saved his life. . . .

"Danger?" he growled. "Hell, it's a damn sight safer on the bottom than it is up here!"

"I heard about it," the doctor said dryly. "But you can talk about that later, too. Just relax, now. And keep this oxygen mask on for awhile."

After a time, the doctor went out through the air lock, leaving the pharmacist's mate to watch over the big patient and to continue rubbing his arms and legs. The nitrogen was gradually working off; oxygen speeded the action of his blood in getting rid of the gas. The pressure inside the chamber was reduced at carefully timed intervals.

Mike could think, now. He reviewed the whole mysterious train of events, from the time the *Starfish* started her full crash diving test to the present. McQuaid, clubbed to death as he lay unconscious after the operation on his fractured skull . . . young John Thorpe prowling about the hospital grounds in the rainy dark, carrying a billiard cue. . . .

"Doc," Mike asked the pharmacist's mate, "did you ever have any experience with a sleepwalker?"

There was still enough pressure in the chamber to distort a man's voice. The corpsman looked up quickly.

"With a what? A streetwalker?"

"No, no—sleepwalker! A guy who walks around with his eyes open, but who is really caulking off!"

The pharmacist's mate chuckled, then sobered. "Knew one once, at the San Diego hospital. He got a medical survey out of the Navy. They figured they couldn't take chances on a man who might get out of his hammock some night and stroll over the side."

"That's what this kid is supposed to have done," Mike Way said. "It's not a gag, then?"

"Oh, absolutely not—I mean, not if the guy who does it ain't putting on a gag! I guess it would be kind of hard to tell whether a man was faking, or not. Anyway, this bird got out of the Navy that way. But I've seen a few others try to work tricks to get paid off, and it made me kind of suspicious. One guy faked a pretty good TB cough, and when he was ordered up for an X-ray of his chest, he soaked some cigarettes in iodine and smoked them—figuring the smoke would color his lungs enough that they'd photograph dark, like they were inflamed."

"Did they give him a survey?"

"I don't know," the corpsman said. "I was shanghaied to the battle-wagons about that time. Oh, if a man really wants out of the Service, they might as well kick him out—he's no good in the Navy!"

Mike Way lay digesting this. He couldn't imagine anybody's wanting out of the Navy. But, then, some men couldn't stand the gaff. That first six months or a year—training station drills, messcook duty, and all the really tough parts. He could remember his own days as an apprentice and second class seaman, and the thought came to him suddenly that young John Thorpe was not yet through that trying period.

But he pulled his mind back to the present, and the problem before him. Regardless of who was guilty of the murders, there was that thing he had seen projecting from one of the vents in the conning tower of the *Starfish*. It looked, Mike Way recalled, something like the blade of a thin, curved knife.

He said, "I don't see how another dive would hurt me! Before they had recompression tanks, didn't they send a guy back down to the bottom and bring him up more slowly? The pressure down there's the same as here!"

"Except," supplied the pharmacist's mate, "you get oxygen here, and CO_2 down there. And up here you're warm and dry, and you're not going to slip and fall twenty feet off a deck and get squeezed completely into your helmet! No, I'd say there's a slight difference!"

Back in Admiral Wetherbee's room, Evelyn Brill and Vince Ayres were looking at a chart the gaunt old man had drawn with no small amount of draughtsman's skill.

"Submarines have changed considerably since I did duty in them," he said in his booming voice. "But I went over this with Lieutenant James, and it's fairly accurate. You see this, doctor?"

He pointed with his pencil to lines on the chart. Vince nodded. "But human anatomy and the complications of a submarine are two different things," the doctor said. "I don't understand it."

"The *Starfish*," explained the Admiral, "had two separate main induction systems to supply air when she was on the surface. They were separate, mind you. Both opened up here. The bigger induction ran aft—that's where the Diesels were, and, naturally, they had to have more air back there."

"I can see that," Evelyn said.

"All right. When making preparations for a dive, the power is shifted to the electric motors. The inductions are closed. You can't see the valves, up there, but there is an indicator board that lights up— red and green. It's in the control room, and they call it the 'Christmas tree.' Lieutenant James, your father, and several other men have told me that the Christmas tree's lights were all green. So—" and the Admiral sighed, "—the vents were closed. I had thought perhaps the water came in there. . . ."

Vince Ayres rose and impatiently paced the room. "Then that leads us nowhere!" he said, stopping to face the Admiral. "Mike Way found something, but it could hardly be those valves you've sketched—they certainly couldn't be seen from the outside of the ship."

"He may have discovered a break in the hull," the Admiral said. "Or a hatch open aft—one of many things."

"Well, we'll find out when he's sufficiently recovered to return to the *Consolation*," Vince went on. "But in the meantime, we've got to act! Before somebody else is murdered!"

Admiral Wetherbee shook his head with a mysterious half smile, and pressed the buzzer. He said: "There will be no more murders, doctor. Not so long as Mike Way is out of reach. And when he comes back to the ship—oh, corpsman, do you think you could forage the icebox and find me a turkey leg? Thank you. And when he comes back to the ship, we must see that he's safely locked up."

A sudden thought struck Evelyn. She leaned forward to look the shaggy-browed man squarely in the eyes.

"Did you have anything to do with Dad's arrest, Admiral Wetherbee?"

"Well, yes," nodded the Admiral. "I sent a recommendation to the Commandant just before we sailed, urging that Lieutenant Brill be placed in custody—protective custody. The Commandant approved and radio orders to that effect followed."

Angry color flooded the girl's cheeks, but her voice was cold. "You surely must have known what this means to his record at a time when he's being considered for selection as lieutenant commander! It might have even—"

"Just a minute, Evelyn," the Admiral said quietly. "I'm sure there'll be no entry on his service record. Let me tell you why I took that course of action. Now, when we came aboard the *Consolation*, I reasoned that Thorpe was not the murderer. I deduced that Everett Brill was either guilty of murder, or he was in danger of being killed, himself. No—hear me out, now! McQuaid was killed to cover up something. It could have been neglect of duty on your father's part—the intoxication charge, which I didn't want to believe—or it could have been to cover up any chance of a structural fault's being discovered before Westco Iron Works cinched that fat government contract."

"So you took it out on Dad," Evelyn said bitterly. She was dangerously near to tears.

"No. I had him locked up to eliminate him from the scene, both for his own protection and to study what happened. You know how well my theory was proved—much more strongly than I'd expected—by Cardoni's murder."

"And that helped Dad a lot!" the girl cried. "He was seen in the passageway just before Cardoni's body was found!"

"That was a coincidence," the Admiral said. "Oh, you may hate me now for having had Lieutenant Brill locked up. But it was the best thing to do. I wish, now, that we had locked up Cardoni."

The corpsman came back with a turkey leg and a glass of milk, and grinned as he put the platter on the bedside locker. The Admiral began eating.

Vince Ayres sat down again. He said, "Well—what about Thorpe, then? Is he missing, or not?"

Admiral Wetherbee's sea-blue eyes twinkled and then turned crafty. "You've certainly got me under your guns tonight, haven't you?" he chuckled. "Well . . . I don't know where Thorpe is. I haven't seen him since I had him up here for questioning. Did they search the ship thoroughly?"

"Yes, sir," Vince answered.

"They found his white hat and some of his clothes, I'm told," the Admiral went on. "That looks bad. The lad most certainly should have been locked up, doctor."

"I've been criticized on that point!" Vince snapped. "You questioned him, then. What did you learn?"

The Admiral's brows crawled together. "I found out more by having information relayed to me from ashore data concerning his life as a civilian. You were right when you speculated that he'd been somewhat of a mamma's boy. Only son of a widowed mother. Three older sisters. Spoiled and petted—you might say he had an apron-string complex, and the Navy was too much for him."

"He might have changed," Evelyn said. "The transition to submarine life was too sudden. And the shock he suffered! I've never been able to convince myself that he had anything to do with the murders."

"I think his connection with the case was quite similar to your father's," the Admiral said. "So far as our investigation, I mean. He could have been considered guilty. On the other hand, he himself was the most logical contender for the doubtful honor of becoming the next victim, because with his death all three of the men who escaped from the after portion of the *Starfish* would have been silenced. He must have known this, and it preyed upon his mind. So—he disappeared, and we have reasonable proof that he wasn't guilty, now. That proof is the fact that the murderer subsequently tried to kill Mike Way."

Vince shook his head. "In other words, you eliminated Brill, and you're of the opinion that Thorpe eliminated himself. And then the murderer still strikes—at the man who thinks he's found why the *Starfish* sank. You're intimating, then, that one of four persons committed the murders!"

"What four?" the Admiral asked mildly.

"Martin West, Victor Melhorne, Foster Bedell or Barbara West! Oh, I've had my suspicions, too, but we haven't an iota of real evidence against any of them! We're right where we started!"

"I'm not intimating any of them is guilty," the Admiral denied. "They built that ship; it seems to me that sabotage by any of them—and that's what you'd have to consider—would be very unlikely. But there are others. Did you question Kowalski?"

"Why, yes, briefly. He wasn't aft in the submarine, and he certainly had no reason to kill McQuaid or Cardoni."

The Admiral reached for his logbook. From the number of pages he turned before finding what he sought, Vince realized that the old man had made public only a fraction of his entries.

"I had Kowalski's past investigated, too," he said. "Listen. 'Kowalski, Ivan Peter, Fireman 1c, USN. From Chicago. Father was a radical. Kowalski himself once active in Young Communist group. Arrested once on charge of arson, but acquitted. Apparently reformed in political beliefs and joined Navy. Navy record good.'"

Vince said, "You don't mean to tell me you think anybody would attempt to destroy a submarine when he was down in it!"

"I never knew a man so foolish," the Admiral sighed.

"All right, sir," Vince replied, and came to the point. "That logbook has been of great help, so far, Admiral. But today, in it, you said you knew the identity of the murderer. That's what I came here to find out—if you do know, this is no time to be keeping the knowledge secret!"

The Admiral's hearty chuckle rumbled through the room. "Doctor," he said with an airy wave of the diminished drumstick, "I wouldn't want you to pass this along. Nor you, Evelyn. Both of you know how scuttlebutt rumor spreads through a ship . . ."

They were expectantly silent. Admiral Wetherbee permitted himself another chuckle.

"The fact is," he said, "that logbooks sometimes give out the damnedest false impressions to be found anywhere!"

"Then you really don't know!" Vince accused.

The Admiral looked at the porthole as if his keen old eyes could see the rise and fall of the swells that were one with the darkness. He said, evasively: "Did you ever hear the old story about the merchant skipper and the mate who was inclined to tipple now and then? The skipper logged this entry: 'The mate was drunk today.' That made the mate pretty sore, being put on record. Next day, when he had occasion to write the log, he put down: 'The captain was sober today.'"

He smiled at them innocently. "That shows you. I'd like to create the illusion that this logbook sees, knows and tells all—and I'd like you to help me create that illusion. But, as for yourselves, remember that any logbook can give out a false impression!"

18
IRISH PENNANTS

Vince Ayres hardly knew whether to be angry or amused when he and Evelyn left the Admiral's room. Humor of the situation struck him, but he felt a certain annoyance, too. The Commandant had placed him in charge of the investigation, but this old man lay back in his quiet room with his starboard leg in a cast, and pulled the strings as if all the actors in the grim mystery play were puppets.

They stopped in a ward diet kitchen, where Mae Kennedy, the prematurely motherly-looking nurse, made them coffee and sandwiches and remarked that they must be dead on their feet.

Evelyn shook her head, and Vince saw a glint in her gray eyes. She told him, when Mae was out of hearing, "I'm not tired anymore! I'm angry—and disappointed. The Admiral has always been one of my favorite people. But what right did he have to cause Dad's arrest—to cause him all the mental torture he's suffered for two days?"

"I don't know," Vince said slowly. He removed his glasses, and she noticed how much younger his sensitive face looked without them. He said, "Maybe he was right, though, Evelyn. Better a little mental discomfort than a shot in the back—or a marlin hitch around your neck!"

"Oh, I don't question his motives. He thought he was doing the right thing. But you're in charge, Vince, and—well, I trust your judgment. If you'd had Dad locked up—"

She stopped, confused. Vince Ayres reached for her hand, and their eyes met, shining. But the plump nurse came back into the diet kitchen to sterilize a hypodermic needle, and the shadow of unsolved and unknown things rose between them.

"You're in charge," Evelyn repeated. "After all, he's retired, and his rank doesn't count so much anymore. We'd all appreciate his help, of course, but he's practically taken things over—and bungled them! He's claimed publicly that the crime is solved. And he can't make good on that claim!"

"I wonder?" Vince said softly. "The old boy is very shrewd. . . . I can understand how he feels, too, Evelyn. By the time a man reaches flag rank, he's pretty well accustomed to running his own show. So, the Admiral has been virtually running this one behind the scenes. But maybe he saved your father from getting killed—we'll probably never know. Let's give him a little more time to make good before we pass judgment. After all, I've accomplished nothing—and I've only got twenty-four more hours to figure this thing out!"

"But suppose you haven't turned up the murderer by tomorrow night? What can Captain McKee do about it? He doesn't know the background of the case. He'd be starting in cold!"

"He wouldn't start on it at all," Vince said grimly. "He'd simply lock all of us up—you and me, too—and keep us locked up until we've docked again, and authorities ashore can take over. That way, the murder trail would be getting colder all the time, and none of us could help."

When Vince had gone to his room, Lieutenant James came looking for him. The small, dapper officer didn't look like a man who'd gone through an ordeal of waiting on the bottom of the sea, but his eyes were worried. After some hesitation, he drew a bottle from his pocket.

"Chief Way sent word down by the rescue bell that you wanted to see this, doctor," he said. "But if somebody's trying to tell you the skipper was drunk, that somebody's a liar!"

Vince smiled at this straightforward expression of loyalty. "I don't think it will come to that now," he assured James. "But this bottle may be Exhibit A for the defense if Everett Brill should be accused."

He drew the cork to smell and taste the few drops of liquid remaining in the small flask.

"Elixir of terpin hydrate, all right," he said. "Cough medicine. I think maybe somebody jogged the pharmacist's mate's elbow when he poured in the alcohol. But a man would have to drink a considerable quantity to get tight on it."

"I'm glad I brought the bottle up, then," James said. "I was worried when the chief said you wanted it. You see, doctor, Captain Brill is—well, a white man! He's Four-O. And all of us are back of him. All of us," he added significantly, "who are left."

"I can't say what will happen if the board of inquiry has to investigate a submarine disaster and several murders, too," Vince said. "But I'm hoping he won't be blamed for anything. I'd like to ask you a few questions, Lieutenant."

The executive officer could tell him nothing new. Yes, he had noticed McQuaid's bitterness toward the captain—like Mike Way, he thought it was one of those things Everett Brill could handle, and it would have adjusted itself within a short time. A shakedown cruise, James said, not only proved a ship's engines, but it got the personnel working smoothly, too. He agreed that Cardoni was wrought up to the point of murder after McQuaid shut that watertight door.

"But the chances were that Cardoni's brother never could have reached the door, anyway," he said, and the memory of the horror twisted his lips. "Those men back there died quickly and mercifully."

"What about Thorpe?" Vince asked.

"He was one of those problem children who get in the Navy now and then. He should have been given an inaptitude discharge at the training station. Maybe that sounds harsh. I've seen some of those boys snap out of it and make sailormen, all right. But I'm not sure that Thorpe ever would have done that. I expected to see him go over the hill—run away—the first time he had liberty and a few dollars."

"Do you think he'd be capable of committing a couple of murders—and trying a third?"

James stared. "I don't get that—about the third attempt," he said. "Not if you mean the shots fired at Mike Way. Thorpe disappeared before that happened, according to what I was told—walked over the side!"

"I'm only speculating," Vince said. "What do you think?"

"Hell! I think it takes a certain amount of nerve to commit a murder!"

Vince undressed as soon as the submarine's executive officer had gone. Then he answered a knock at his door, and received a radio message from the Intelligence officer on shore:

RADIO NINETEENTH NAVAL THIRTEENTH 0120 BT
LIEUT. VINCENT AYRES USS CONSOLATION BT
MCQUAID MURDER WEAPON FOUND LATE YES-
TERDAY AFTERNOON BY MAN CLIPPING HEDGE
BELOW BALCONY IT WAS BRICK WHICH HAD
BEEN USED AS SHOCK BLOCK TO ELEVATE FOOT
OF HOSPITAL BED MATE TO IT FOUND IN CLOS-
ET OF VACANT NUMBER THREE QUIET ROOM
INDICATING MURDERER WENT THROUGH THAT
ROOM TO GAIN ACCESS TO BALCONY MICRO-
SCOPIC AND CHEMICAL EXAMINATION OF BRICK
SHOWS BLOODSTAINS ALSO LINT FROM NURSES
CAPE IN WHICH IT WAS WRAPPED BT
SIMMONS
TOD 0128

Vince went to bed with his head whirling from weariness and a sense of confusion. Nothing tied in here to make a complete pattern; the case was full of seemingly irrelevant things, such as the Admiral's deduction that the murder blows had been timed to the chopping of ice in the diet kitchen. Everything was at loose ends. Admiral Wetherbee, he reflected, would have called these dangling, unsecured pieces of evidence "Irish pennants." The investigation appeared to be becalmed, fouled in a Sargasso sea of complications and possibilities.

John Thorpe was as James had described him—he had lacked the nerve required to commit murder. Initiative, Vince thought, was a better word. But Thorpe normally awake and Thorpe as a somnambulist were two different persons; the subconscious desire to kill might have manifested itself in his sleep.

But the Admiral apparently believed Thorpe was dead before that gun was thrust through a porthole to fire at Mike Way. The *Consolation* was a big ship and an almost empty one; Vince was not overlooking the possibility of a man's being able to hide in it.

He doubted, however, that any somnambulist could aim a gun within inches of a man's head. And when things went back to a rainy night on the hospital balcony, and to a man seen there with a club, they came to a new tangle. The club was irrelevant, too; it had not been the murder weapon.

Irish pennants, and nothing else.

The ship slept. At 0345 the bosun's mate on duty roused out the four-to-eight anchor watch, and a seaman climbed to the bridge with a pot of "jamoke"—the Navy's word for coffee. The *Consolation* was swinging a little with the tide as she rode the dark, lifting swells. There was still a ring around the moon, and from high above the riding lights of the ships standing on the sea—the *Algonquin*, yonder, and the *Westsal* scarcely a line's throw to her starboard, and the *Consolation* and a destroyer anchored a little farther away.

Lights gleamed from the portholes of one room well aft on the main deck of the *Consolation*. The Admiral was writing in his log, chuckling to himself in the full satisfaction of employing Navy terms to record trivial incidents:

USS CONSOLATION, 13 January.

At Sea. Anchored as before.

1400 Making all preparations for going into condition of Readiness No. 2, this date.

0410 to 1530 Asleep.

0535 Admiral J. K. WETHERBEE, USN (Retired) left his bed, boarded wheelchair with two hospital corpsmen as sideboys, breaking his flag as Commander Mechanized Forces Afloat. (Comechfor.)

0536 Shifted to hand steering, experiencing some difficulty occasioned by roll of the ship.

WORK AND DRILL SCHEDULE

USS Wheelchair, 13 January

0540 All hands.

0600 Turn to. Clean shave port and starboard. Dry down by 0610.

0700 Breakfast.

0800 Muster on stations and submit reports of absentees to murder investigating board prior to 0850.

1200 Dinner.

1300 Turn to. Continue navigating wheelchair operating independently. Continue investigation. 1730 Supper.

2030 Go into Condition of Readiness No. 2. All hands battle stations. Darken ship.

2040 (or when Contact is made) Trap murderer and solve tactical problem of murder mystery. Solve mystery of loss of USS STARFISH.

2100 (or as soon as is practicable thereafter) Hoist signal. Cease Present Exercises. Convene critique in isolation ward.

J. K. WETHERBEE

Rear Admiral, U. S. Navy, (Retd.)

COMECHFOR.

If Victor Melhorne could have seen the Admiral as he wrote, the pale-eyed shipbuilding official would have been certain that the old man was, indeed, in his second childhood. But Melhorne was asleep, and he had no inkling of the schedule Admiral Wetherbee had drawn for himself.

Dawn came over the sea, sullen and gray. It was Friday, the thirteenth.

For the rest of those aboard, the day began much as yesterday had started. For Vince Ayres, the outlook was even blacker. But there was a break in the ship's routine.

It came immediately after quarters, and because of its nature it was not listed either on the *Consolation's* Work and Drill Schedule, or on that Admiral Wetherbee had written. General alarm gongs began ringing throughout the ship with their high-tongued, insistent clamor. A bugle blared from the loud speakers, and the swift patter of feet swept over the deck above the isolation ward.

Evelyn Brill caught her breath. There was something ominous in the tempo of these sounds. She turned to Vince Ayres.

"Fire, Vince?"

The bugle was blowing double time. Vince shook his head and smiled to reassure the girl. And then a bosun's pipe shrilled through the speakers, and the bosun's voice followed:

"*All hands abandon ship! All hands abandon ship!*"

"It's just a drill," Vince said. "Come with me! All right, everybody—lay up to your boat stations!"

He seized lifejackets and thrust one into Evelyn's hand. As they ran up the ladder, she noted the swift, synchronized pattern with which the *Consolation's* crew acted: only the four civilians seemed bewildered. Men came up from below to the loud rattling of hand chains; the general alarm gongs were still beating everywhere throughout the ship. As they reached their station near the boat assigned to them, hospital corpsmen appeared bearing stretchers and first-aid pouches.

"There's Dad!" Evelyn cried.

He smiled across at her, but he still looked pale and worried. There was a belted sentry with him. She could guess that this little interlude of make-believe action had stirred him, just as it brought a tingle to her spine. The Navy—the salt of it and the steel of it—was in their blood.

An officer moved swiftly along the deck, inspecting lifebelts, checking the boat crews and equipment. Vince caught Evelyn's arm.

"Look!" he exclaimed.

It was a bareheaded, thin-faced man in undress whites, standing by with the group at the next boat. It was John Thorpe!

The bugle sounded Secure. The bosun's pipe shrilled again, and the voice from all the loud speakers said, "Secure!" A big chief master-at-arms hustled Thorpe below again. But everybody in the murder investigation party had seen him.

Before anybody could go below again, a chief petty officer approached the boat station where Vince stood, and accosted the square-faced, curly headed Kowalski.

"You're detailed to go over to the *Westsal*," he said. "They may want you to dive."

19
LOWER AWAY!

The *Algonquin* tossed uneasily. It was just after noon; the sea had quieted considerably, and the sky was overcast. Big Mike Way sat disconsolately on the bitts while the bears dressed another man. He was a chunky and cheerful second-class gunner's mate named Alexander. Mike Way wasn't going down.

It was no use arguing with the doctor. Or with the three-striper who was in charge of salvage operations.

"I *got* to dive!" the chief torpedoman said. "I got to—it's important. She was my ship. Can't I be the first to open that after hatch and go inside her? I got a right to do that!"

The pharmacist's mate who had spent most of the night in the recompression chamber with him grunted.

"You've got a crow, Tubes," he said, and patted the eagle on Mike's starboard sleeve. "What do you want—a pair of wings?"

"It's as important as hell!" Mike insisted.

Alexander sat on the dressing bench, as nonchalantly as if he were going for a walk. The wind died, and fog came stealthily over the sea's face like a thick gray veil. It blotted out the destroyer, first, and Mike Way watched it swallow the *Consolation* and the *Westsal*. The bears put the heavy shoes on Alexander's feet and lifted the copper breastplate into place. Mike Way saw him feeling for his knife to make certain it was in its sheath.

Then they put his helmet on and helped him to the stage. It wasn't right. Another man doing Mike Way's job. He saw Alexander giving his suit air, and the stage went down to helmet depth in the water.

"Take him to the descending line!"

The bubbles began drifting along the side of the ship in a silvery chain.

"Lower away!"

The commander came along the deck toward Alexander's talker, and Mike Way rose.

"Commander, sir, I—"

"Nothing doing, Chief!" the officer said kindly. "We've got enough divers on the sick list, as it is. We don't want to kill anybody. They've already had Kowalski sent over to the *Westsal* as a spare diver, and there's plenty help."

So it was no use Mike Way sat down again, his shoulders hunched. Sometimes those ribs he had cracked or bruised in the *Starfish* bothered him They were still sore. But, hell, a man felt just as well on the bottom—better than he did up here, knowing that there was something to look for down below.

The talker said, "He's on the submarine. Okay, Alec! Take it easy, now. Get your bearings . . . Okay!"

An interval. Only the slap of the swells against the side, the tautening and slackening of the lines that meant air and life to the diver forty fathoms down. Mike Way was sweating despite the chill fog. He knew every move Alexander would be making, down there. Groping aft. Walking like a man in slow motion pictures, guarding against a misstep that might plunge him over the slippery, rounded side and into a fatal squeeze. Working his way toward that other escape hatch which no man had lived to use. . . .

"He's at the hatch!"

Had to be careful, now, Mike Way thought. If there should be pressure sealed in that portion of the submarine, the hatch might fly open the instant its catch was released. Might knock Alexander over the side. . . .

"He's trying to open it."

The minutes were adding up. Twenty minutes down there at that pressure was enough for anybody. Mike Way looked out into the swirl of gray fog and cursed his luck. If he hadn't got the bends yesterday, they'd have let him dive.

"He's having a little trouble with the hatch!"

Mike Way swabbed the perspiration from his forehead. Everybody on the deck of the *Algonquin* felt the strain. Every man of them was down there, trying to help. . . .

"Alec!" There was a new note in the talker's voice. "Are you okay? Hey, Alec! Answer me—can't you hear me?" And then a strained interval, and "Commander, his phone's gone dead!"

The Commander was taking no chances. He whirled toward the men who handled Alexander's lines. "Take him up!"

They hauled in the slack. It came, and that was all; the next swell put a strain on the lines that wasn't good to see.

"Alec! Sound off, down there! Can you hear me? See if you can get a signal on his lifeline, you guys!"

They yanked on the line, but no answering jerk came. Mike Way got slowly to his feet, wondering what had happened. The after part of the *Starfish* should be free of any gear that might entangle lines. But you never could tell, up here where the sea rolled and the fog was wet to your cheek.

"His lines are fouled, Commander! We can't hoist him!"

"Vast heaving!" the officer said sharply. "We'll have to send another diver down."

Mike Way sprang forward eagerly. "Let me go, sir!" he cried. "I know the ship, Commander—let me go!"

"Get into a rig, Chief!" the Commander said.

Vince Ayres went aft to the Admiral's room immediately after Secure had been sounded following the abandon ship drill. Before, he had been half amused; now he was angry. He knocked, and the booming voice told him to enter.

Admiral Wetherbee was in his wheelchair with the plaster cast thrust straight out on the elevated half of the footrest. He had turned the chair to face the bow of the ship; that way, the beam roll did not disturb its equilibrium. And he was reading Mahan.

"Good morning, doctor!" he said heartily. "I've been expecting you. Anything new?"

"You didn't turn out for abandon ship drill, did you, sir?" Vince asked significantly.

"In this rig? No."

"Well, Thorpe did!"

The Admiral's shaggy gray brows went up. "That so? Everybody saw him, I suppose?"

"Everybody. Including Captain McKee. You told me last night that you didn't know where he was. I've appreciated your help, Admiral Wetherbee, but don't you think that's going a little too far? I reported Thorpe missing. I'm delighted that he isn't, but I think you might have told me—"

The Admiral waved a bony hand. "Captain McKee has already been in to see me!" he said, and chuckled. "Bawled me out—first time I've had rocks and shoals read to me in years. I rather enjoyed it, doctor. It's good for anybody in this man's Navy to have a dressing down now and then. It makes you remember that no matter how much gold you get on your sleeve, there's always someone in authority over you!"

"About Thorpe, now!" Vince reminded him.

"Oh, yes! Well, doctor, if you'll remember, I didn't tell you a lie last night. I said I didn't know where Thorpe was—which was literally true. I left his place of confinement to the chief master-at-arms, who once did duty with me when I was in the battleships. That chief, doctor, would do almost anything I ask."

"Very commendable loyalty, I'm sure!" Vince said with considerable sarcasm. "Your putting Everett Brill out of danger was a good idea, sir. But we knew where Brill was; I could question him if the need for further questioning arose. It was different in Thorpe's case. I wanted to study that boy. I wanted to determine whether his somnambulism was real or faked. And you have him secretly locked up!"

"Just a minute, doctor!" There were storm signals in the old man's eyes. "You will understand, before the day is over, that I saved Thorpe's life by acting as I did. Also, the belief that Thorpe was dead gave the murderer a sense of false security that has helped to draw the net a little tighter."

"I can't see it!" Vince said.

"You will. Sit down, doctor. And look at this. It's a Work and Drill Schedule I've drawn up for today. . . ."

Vince Ayres permitted himself a little snort as he skimmed over the Admiral's fine writing. Friction with this old man was the last thing he would have expected when the *Consolation* put to sea and murder went along with her. But now he had begun to wonder if what Victor Melhorne had said wasn't true. Admiral Wetherbee was in his second childhood.

"2040 (or when Contact is made)," he read. "Trap murderer and solve tactical problem of murder mystery. Solve mystery of loss of USS STARFISH."

He said, aloud: "I'm afraid we're a long way from the goal you've outlined, laudable as it is. You'll excuse me now, sir—I've work to do. I'd like to ask you one thing. Has Thorpe been permitted to leave his room? Did Miss Wilkins actually see him?"

The Admiral chuckled. "When she thought she saw a ghost? Yes, that was Thorpe in the flesh. I had him brought up here for questioning, and I apparently frightened him rather badly. So he was quite pale as he went back. And I had given him a pair of bed sheets—whatever storeroom or gear locker the chief placed him in had no bedding. He went out of here with the sheets draped over his shoulder."

"Then if he had the run of the ship, he could have been the person who fired at Mike Way!"

"Sea dust!" snorted the Admiral. "Thorpe had no gun. I'm sure he wasn't at large at that time. I impressed upon him the necessity for his keeping to his hideout, for his own protection. I also told him he was no more a sleepwalker than I am—and I hardly ever sleep!"

A short time before, this old sailor had been asking Vince to draw upon his medical knowledge in an effort to determine whether Thorpe's sleepwalking was real. It amused the doctor now to find that the Admiral had made his own diagnosis.

"Remember how he jumped when he knocked that glass off this bedside locker?" the Admiral asked. "Well, a man who is asleep certainly wouldn't react so quickly—he'd wait until the tumbler struck his foot!"

Vince had no comment. He only asked, dryly: "What did the boy say?"

"Why, he maintained that he was asleep, of course. But I have my own idea about that. After what's happened, he couldn't very well admit he had been faking."

Vince rose to go. He said, politely: "Admiral Wetherbee, I've appreciated your assistance. But so long as I have been charged with the responsibility of running down this murderer, I must protest against any further interference from any source. Do I make myself clear, sir?"

The Admiral stiffened. "Perfectly, doctor!" he growled.

Those storm signals glinted in his sea-blue eyes again. And as Vince came to attention out of respect for the old man's rank, he thought he saw another light in them. He left with the distinct impression that Admiral J. K. Wetherbee was secretly laughing.

And when he had gone, the man in the wheelchair reached for his buzzer.

"Ask one of the radiomen to step in here a moment, please!" he told the corpsman who answered. And while he was waiting, he added one of the personal entries that had become so numerous in his logbook of late:

> NOTE: Admirable spirit shown by Lieut Vincent AYRES, (MC) USN. Not always found in staff officers. Forced to conclusion that nothing is holding him back so far as BRILL, Evelyn, NNC, is concerned, except her determination not to marry a Navy man. Must talk to her again about this.

Vince Ayres went to the isolation ward where the other members of the party had gathered. The first person he saw as he entered the door was Captain McKee. The tall, military-looking medical officer was accompanied by the chief master-at-arms, and just now he wore an exceptionally grim countenance.

"We've been waiting for you for some time, Dr. Ayres!" McKee said snappishly. "This isn't getting the murder mystery cleared away, you know."

More interference, Vince thought. The Commandant might have expected it would work out this way, when he sent a medical corps two-striper to sea in charge of an investigation. He was suddenly weary of the job, sick of the whole case. He looked past McKee and saw Martin West's face reflecting an enjoyment of his discomfiture, and there was a superior disdain on Barbara West's magenta lips. But Evelyn Brill met his glance with warm sympathy in her gray eyes, and he knew that she understood.

Captain McKee's next words brought him back to the present, and to a quick, heightened interest.

"You may wonder just why I chose to hold abandon ship drill this morning," the captain was saying. "While it was going on, a thorough search was being made of all quarters. We found this."

He held out an object wrapped in medical department gauze. The white folds fell away from the cold glint of blue steel.

"The gun," McKee said, "that was fired at Mike Way!"

Vince Ayres scarcely heard these words. He was listening to a fluttery little cry that broke through the ward as everyone craned their necks to see what the captain was holding.

The sound escaped from the lips of Barbara West.

Captain McKee faced her. "Yes, Miss West," he said slowly, "the gun was in your room. Perhaps you can explain its possession."

For a space, there was strained, tense silence in the compartment. The *Consolation* lifted on a swell, slanted down with it, and lurched slightly in the trough. From the deck forward, the shrill of a bosun's pipe came dimly, and a faintly heard shout of "Sweepers, start your brooms! Give her a clean sweep down, fore and aft!" But here in the isolation ward, there was no movement.

Vince Ayres looked at the smartly dressed girl. Her lips moved, but no sound came from them. She buried her face suddenly in her hands. And then Martin West was on his feet, his heavy features at first pale, then darkening under an angry rush of color.

"This is preposterous, Captain McKee!" he shouted. "If the gun was found there, it had been planted! My daughter never owned a pistol in her life—I doubt that she ever shot one!"

The captain walked to the ward dressing table where an array of bottles and instruments stood, and carefully put down the gauze-wrapped weapon.

"We will, of course, be able to bring out fingerprints," he said. "The gun was quite cleverly hidden—from a landman's point of view. It had been placed well inside the mouth of the blower. Like this one here," and he indicated the megaphone shaped ventilator on the overhead, "the blower was covered with gauze to prevent any soot from being blown into the room. It might have been found today, anyway, because the gauze is changed every Friday. But I instructed the searching party to look inside the blowers. They happen to be favorite hiding places for liquor, non-regulation clothing, and anything else a hospital corpsman isn't supposed to have in his possession."

West made an angry gesture. "That's all beside the point! I say the gun must have been planted there. It was put where it *would* be found, so as to divert suspicion from the man who's guilty. If it wasn't, why didn't he merely throw it over the side?"

Vince Ayres said, "Perhaps I can answer that. Perhaps the person who fired it—and missed, remember—intended to use it again. Guns aren't plentiful aboard a hospital ship, you know. The *Consolation* is a non-combatant—she has no armory."

He faced Barbara West. All her spoiled pride and hauteur were gone; she was a pitiful huddle, now, shaken by frightened sobs.

"Miss West—" he began.

"I—I never saw the thing before!" she wailed, lifting her head. Mascara had streaked her cheeks, and her eyes were wide and scared. "I don't know anything about it! Please leave me alone—leave me alone!"

Martin West took her in his arms, and glared defiantly at the Navy men. Captain McKee glanced significantly at Vince Ayres. Both were remembering that Barbara had cried out the instant the gun was unwrapped. Both knew she was lying.

"Dr. Ayres," McKee said, "I'll take the gun to the laboratory and have the fingerprints brought out and photographed. You will please carry on. Oh—here's the clip taken from the gun. Three cartridges gone." He turned at the door, and added: "Please remember that I expect action today!"

20
"I WANT TO CONFESS!"

Mike Way frowned over the side of the *Algonquin* as the bears made record time hustling him into his diving suit. Bubbles were still swinging to the heaving surface in a slender, silvery chain—Alexander was still getting air, unless there was a leak in his line. But all efforts to hoist him had failed, and the deck crew didn't dare pull any harder for fear of breaking the precious air hose.

The commander who was in charge of the salvage operations came to the dressing bench, looking worried.

"You understand how to operate the underwater torch, Way," he said. "Better take it down with you. It may be necessary to cut something away. Alexander's got quite a bit of line out—he may have entered the submarine before getting caught!"

"Aye, aye, sir!" Mike Way said.

They weighted him with shoes and belt, got the breastplate collar over his wide shoulders, and nearly tore off his nose putting the helmet over his head in a hurry. But he cursed them for their slowness; it seemed an age before the face port was closed and he could test his air.

He opened the valve over his left breast. There was a hiss and a roar; the breastplate lifted, and the rubberized canvas suit filled, making Mike Way formidable. He felt down at his side for the copper sheath, and made sure that his knife was in place.

"Test your phone, Mike," the talker said.

"One, two, three, four!" Mike said impatiently.

"Okay!"

Somebody rapped twice on the resounding copper helmet with a wrench. Mike turned, shuffling toward the stage with two men to help him. His ribs were sore. It required effort to pull himself onto the swaying stage and grasp the bails with his mittened hands.

The gray water lapped over his leaden shoes. Going down. His helmet went under, and the stage stopped with a jerk. Mike tested the air again, and valved out the extra pressure by hitting the spit-valve with his chin. No leaks in the suit. The exhaust valve at the back of his helmet was gurgling merrily.

"Okay—ready for the torch!" he said.

It came snaking down before him, suspended by the hoses which supplied air, oxygen and hydrogen, and the wire for the electric igniter. Mike Way thrust his left arm through a lanyard on the torch, and called for them to take him to the descending line.

His ribs hurt as the pressure built up inside his suit. But he felt fine. He was diving again; they should have let him go down in the first place. Once on the bottom, he'd get Alexander out of the jam in a hurry, and start him on his way to topside and safety. Then he could lower himself into the after escape hatch of the *Starfish*.

There was a mystery down below—waiting to be found was the explanation of why the submarine sank so swiftly, and why twenty-two men had died. It was linked, too, with the mystery of two murders or more, and with those shots which came so near to ending Mike Way's own life. He was confident that he would solve at least part of the mystery this trip.

"How do you feel, Mike?" his talker asked.

"Okay. But give me more slack—pay it out faster! Hell, man, I'm in a hurry!"

(Extract from Admiral Wetherbee's log.)
0958 Dispatched urgent priority in code to Commandant Nineteenth Naval.

1035 Learned .32 caliber automatic pistol which was used in attempt to kill WAY, Michael, CTM, has been found in room of WEST, Barbara. Is she still attempting to protect someone? Or has she been protecting, all along, her father's chances at a contract to build more than a hundred million dollars worth of submarines? Have no jurisdiction as of present, over civilians in this case.

Must depend upon Lieut. AYRES to question her.

1200 Dinner.

1300 All preparations completed for going into Condition of Readiness No. 2.

Vince Ayres was questioning both Barbara West and her father. It was virtually useless, he had decided, to attempt to glean any information from the girl alone at this time; she probably would become hysterical and cling to her denial that she knew nothing about the gun. And Vince had no taste for third degree tactics.

He sketched the story Barbara had told before for them.

"You will understand, of course, that it is necessary to pry into your private lives more than I like to do," he began politely.

"I'm afraid I *don't* understand!" Martin West said stiffly. "We are not Navy personnel. If police were handling this case, my attorneys would answer the questions—not we!"

"I'm not so sure about that, Mr. West. At any rate, the police aren't handling it. Now, Miss West has told us that she went out on the balcony at the hospital the night of McQuaid's murder. She wore Miss Brill's cape, to protect her clothing from the rain. She attempted to wake Victor Melhorne, at his window, to tell him you were leaving for the hotel. When—"

"We've been through all this!" the dark-haired girl flared.

"When she failed," Vince went on patiently, "she started back to the reception room, and was frightened by a man carrying a club."

"The murderer," said Martin West. "And if you think you're telling me something I don't know, you're wrong. I know my daughter is engaged to marry Victor."

"Did you, at the time?"

"Well, no. But that's beside the point. It was the murderer she saw—the man with the club!"

"Not likely, Mr. West. I haven't told you, but the actual murder weapon was found yesterday at the hospital. It wasn't a club. It was a brick taken from that vacant quiet room—the one between McQuaid's room and the diet kitchen."

Barbara West made an impatient gesture. "But what's the sense of all this? What are you driving at now?"

"This, Miss West," Vince said. He leaned forward, his eyes inscrutable behind his clear glasses. "You've been trying to protect Mr. Melhorne. Under the circumstances, that's natural. But—"

"Protect him?" the girl shot back at Vince. "Against what?"

"Against the suspicion—which *you* have shared, too—that he may have killed Lieutenant McQuaid!"

The shot hit home. Barbara West's laugh was strained, exaggerated. She said, scornfully: "That's silly! Why would Victor have any reason to kill anybody—particularly Lieutenant McQuaid?"

"McQuaid and Mr. Melhorne had an argument," Vince said, and watched Martin West. "McQuaid didn't believe the *Starfish* design was good. He was writing an article saying so. It would have hurt Westco."

Martin West grew livid and loud. "I've had enough of this! I'll go see the Captain!"

"Go ahead," Vince told him grimly. "The Captain has said unless this thing is cleared up tonight, he's going to lock all of us up, and turn the matter over to shore authorities. I can promise you they'd be tougher!"

West subsided. Vince glanced at Evelyn, who was taking notes in shorthand. There was an odd gleam of triumph in his eyes.

"All right," he said. "You'll agree Melhorne would have been pretty anxious to keep that article out of print. Suppose—just suppose, now—that there was a weakness in the design, and McQuaid had discovered it back there in the after portion of the *Starfish*. It's a possible motive. You protected Melhorne before, Miss West, by affirming that he was soundly asleep. Are you doing the same thing now? Is that Victor Melhorne's gun?"

"I've told you I never saw the gun before!" she answered.

"Why don't you ask Lieutenant Brill about the gun?" Martin West demanded. "And that boy—Thorpe! It's odd how he makes people think he was lost over the side, then turns up on deck. You know he was angry at McQuaid."

"Is it *your* gun, Mr. West?" Vince shot at him.

"It is not!"

"Very well. I'll talk to Melhorne and Bedell when they come back from the *Westsal*. By that time we'll have the fingerprint photos. You don't object, of course, to allowing your own fingerprints to be taken for comparison?"

"I certainly do!" the shipbuilder said. "We're not common criminals even if you do seem to think we are!"

"Think it over," Vince advised. "That's all now. Thank you."

He lighted a cigarette and looked thoughtfully through the glass into the ward. There was nobody out there he wanted to question, just now. Thorpe—he'd have Thorpe brought up later from his hiding place, wherever it was. Melhorne he'd have to face later. Bedell didn't tie in. He remembered with a sort of shock that he'd have to ask Evelyn's father more questions: the confinement of both Everett Brill and John Thorpe had not been close enough. If a man could come up to see the Admiral, he might be out of his locked room long enough to attempt a murder.

Evelyn said, "Vince, it's not a Navy gun," and he knew what she was thinking.

"No. But there's nothing to prevent a Navy man from obtaining a gun like it. And it's small enough to be smuggled aboard easy enough. Like sailors sometimes hide a pint bottle in their socks, under their bell-bottoms."

"Whose do you think it is?"

"We may never learn that," he said. "But it's a cinch Barbara West knew it was hidden in her room. She yelled before she was hurt. One thing you have to hand to her—she must really be in love with that pale-eyed Victor Melhorne! She certainly was afraid that he'd committed murder, and she still cared enough to do everything she could to protect him."

"Woman-like," said Evelyn.

He looked at her with a strange tenderness, wondering if she would do the same.

"Any woman," she said softly, "will do her best to reform her man by words and prayers and exemplary righteousness. Up to a certain point, she'll moralize. After that—"

Vince smiled. "Go on," he said.

"That point is danger for her man. When he actually is in peril, she quits preaching. She'd lie and cheat—she'd even kill to save him! That's the way women are, and Barbara West is no different from the rest."

He leaned close, seeing the warm pastel tint creeping into her cheeks because of his nearness. He said, lightly: "Evelyn, if you could love me like that, I'd take your word for it—I'd promise never to commit murder, arson or even mayhem to put you to the test. And as for bigamy, why—I'd only commit bigamy under one circumstance!"

She laughed. He remembered that it had been a long time since he had heard the happiness of her laughter. It never occurred to him that for days he had been serious and worried and driven, or that in his banter he was revealing an almost new side of his nature to the girl.

"All right, Vince!" she prompted. "You'd commit bigamy if—"

"If I found you had a twin sister! Won't you marry me, darling? Oh, a medical officer's duty isn't so bad, Evelyn—not as bad as other Navy people catch. About four years of shore duty to two years at sea. And I'd even consider resigning and entering civil practice."

Somebody laughed out in the ward. Evelyn exclaimed: "Let go my hand, Vince. They're watching us!"

For a moment, enchanted at what they saw in each other's eyes, they had forgotten. The spell was broken, now. There remained a grim task to do. There was the prospect of ruin for her father; there was danger for each of them, and for all the others but one person.

They still had to find out who that person was.

In mid-afternoon, a first class pharmacist's mate came from the laboratory with the pistol. He shook his head as he handed Vince the gun.

"I'm sorry, sir," he said. "Whoever used this roscoe was mighty careful. All the fingerprints had been wiped off. All but one."

"One's all we need!" Vince said. "Did you get that?"

The technician grinned. "Yes, sir. It was the skipper's—Captain McKee's. I compared it with those on his service record, Dr. Ayres."

Vince was too disturbed to appreciate the joke. "Well," he sighed, "that's that. Another blind trail. I suppose all we've got to work on now is the gun's serial number. It looks like a new weapon. I'll send the serial number ashore and see if they can locate the dealer who sold it."

"That's already been done, doctor," said the corpsman. "The Admiral. He sent to the laboratory for a full description and the serial number, then he radioed the dope to somebody in Nineteenth Naval District."

"Thank you, anyway," Vince said.

All along, he thought, there probably had been a duplication of effort—the Admiral likely had been requesting the same information from Intelligence that Vince had asked. Well, the old boy was one up on him, now. Vince made a mental note to call on the Admiral later to ask if any answer had been received to his query concerning the purchase of the automatic.

But another radio message came first. It was an urgent priority for Captain McKee, and the tall four-striper himself brought it to the isolation ward. He appeared visibly disturbed.

"I—er—have received orders which affect you and this—er—group," he said. "With your permission, doctor, I'll read them aloud." He cleared his throat, waited for attention, and then went directly into the main portion of the message:

"'FROM: Commandant, Nineteenth Naval District.
To: Capt. W. P. McKee (MC) USN, Commanding USS *Consolation*.

SUBJECT: Murder inquiry, change in command of.

1. Immediately upon receipt of these orders, Rear Admiral J. K. Wetherbee, USN (Retd.) will assume command of the inquiry into the murders of Lieutenant McQuaid and Machinist's Mate Cardoni, replacing Lieut. Vincent Ayres, (MC) USN.

2. Lieut. Ayres will continue actively in the investigation, rendering all possible assistance to Admiral Wetherbee.

3. Particular effort is to be directed along the lines set forth in the log which Admiral Wetherbee has kept, and which is of the utmost importance in this investigation.'"

There was a silence. Vince broke it by saying, "I will report to the Admiral at once, sir!" He saw resentment blazing in Evelyn Brill's eyes, and Captain McKee drew him aside.

"I want you to know that I made no report, no recommendation," he said. "This is an order, and we shouldn't question it. But what can the Admiral do, doctor? He's an old man, and, what's more, he's got a broken leg and can't get around. If the *Consolation* had been assigned to the Fleet, this wouldn't have happened. The C. in C. wouldn't be putting anybody like the Admiral in charge! It's what comes of being attached to a short district."

Vince smiled, and he wasn't entirely unhappy at the order. He had an idea that somebody—and it could be no one but the Admiral himself—had pulled a string to forestall Captain McKee's threat to lock up everybody and turn the investigation over to the naval authorities ashore. The Admiral had rank enough to get away with such a move; he was retired, and there could be no come-back that would injure him.

"It doesn't really matter," Vince said. "I suppose the Commandant lost patience. And with two murders and a third attempt, the case attained proportions commensurate with flag rank. Frankly, I'll be rather glad to get out from under!"

A messenger entered and handed Vince a folded paper. He opened it and saw a penciled, schoolboy scrawl:

"*Doctor Ayres:*
I have been thinking things over since the Admiral
talked to me. If you can help me by seeing that they
are not too hard on me, I would like to confess.
JOHN THORPE, SEA. 2C"

21
DEATH ON THE BOTTOM

The pressure bit into Mike Way's rugged body. It drove hard against his sore ribs with each of his quickening breaths; it hammered his eardrums and made his head whirl with a weakness he had not known possessed him. He swallowed hard a dozen times, his ears going: "kaloomph!" with each constriction of his throat. It sounded in his head the way a railway trestle sounds inside the train whipping past at express speed.

He looked down as much as his helmet and the bulky air-filled suit would allow, and made out the length of the *Starfish*—a dark, whale-like shadow that straggled into the blue-green dimness. His feet jarred on the duckboards.

"On deck!" he reported in his telephone, "I'm on the submarine!"

"Okay, Mike!" the talker answered. "Take it slow, now—take it slow and get your bearings!"

"Slow, hell!" said Mike Way. He loosened his grip on the descending line, and turned aft with sure direction, peering along the dimness of the whaleback hull for Alexander. But there was no sign of the stocky diver.

Mike Way reported this to the *Algonquin*. The talker said: "He's still getting air. Is that hatch open?"

"What's that?" Mike asked. His voice was flat and queerly distorted by the pressure that roared into his helmet; he throttled down his air for a few seconds so he could hear the man on deck and not a meaningless jumble. Immediately, he felt his breast plate slam against his chest, shooting a spasm of pain through those injured ribs.

The talker repeated.

"Tell you in a minute!" Mike said. He gave himself air again, and leaned against the current. A goggle-eyed fish brushed across his face port.

"I'm getting close to the hatch, now. I can't see anything."

Then he stopped. Alexander wasn't in sight. But yonder were his life line and air hose—the slender threads upon which any diver's life is suspended. They straggled over the side, beyond the hatch—down toward the bottom!

Mike Way felt the chill of the sea, then, driving into his blood and bone. He could sense what had happened. A misstep of a few inches on this slippery deck—a fall over the side. Twenty feet and more to the mud.

Twenty feet didn't seem like much when you were already two hundred and forty down. But it was enough to increase the pressure sharply and suddenly. So much that unless a man had time to shoot more air into his suit to counteract the increase, the "squeeze" got him.

There had been men whose bodies were compressed to pulp and forced into the small globular space of their unyielding helmets by such squeezes. . . .

He said, "I see his lines, now! He must have fallen over the side, well aft. Near the stern planes!" And the pressure took all the tense drama out of his words and made them flat.

He valved down his air and heard the talker ask: "Can you reach him?"

"Minute!" said Mike Way.

He worked his way swiftly, risking a slip himself. The railing ended; Mike grasped the fore-and-aft line that angled down to the stern of the *Starfish*, and leaned out to look over the side.

He still couldn't see Alexander. Perhaps the current had swept him under the rounded hull. His lines wavered down into the deeper dusk that lay along the bottom.

"Looks like his lines are fouled on the stern planes . . . I'm trying to clear them. . . ."

He was hampered by that underwater torch, by all the bulky impedimenta that goes with deep-sea diving. He reached for Alexander's lines and they eluded him; he tried desperately and caught them.

"On deck!" he panted. "Give me some slack!"

Current bent the lines. Mike Way took them forward a few feet.

"On deck! Hoist on Alexander's lines—easy!"

He watched the canvas cover of the lines slide upward a little, then the movement ceased. There was a strain on the lines.

"'Vast heaving!"

He heard the talker repeat the cry. Once more Mike worked frantically The water and the pressure transformed the most frantic haste into agonizing slow motion. . . .

"On deck!" he called. "Try heaving in again. Gently!"

This time the lines kept sliding. Mike heard Alexander's helmet bumping against the hull. A chain of bubbles rose from the exhaust valve. The other diver came slowly into view, and Mike reached out to fend him clear of the submarine.

The instant he touched Alexander's rubberized canvas suit, he knew the man was dead. The suit was filling again as pressure was reduced, but it was still too shrunken for a man of Alexander's stockiness—*it looked almost as if the copper breast plate were touching the suit's back!*

Mike Way looked up, watching a dead man's weighted shoes going aloft. *How many did that make?* Twenty-two in the *Starfish*— two murdered—a diver killed by a squeeze. . . .

"Mike! Are you okay? Sound off, down there!"

Mike Way sounded off with an oath. "Pipe down, damn you!" he said savagely. "Of course I'm okay. Pipe down and leave me alone!"

He moved forward again, holding to the fore-and-aft line, and came to the hatch. It would take him into the after torpedo room, and the engine room was just forward of that. He remembered that thing he had seen in his previous dive—the blade-like object protruding from a vent in the conning tower. But it must have come from the inside of the *Starfish*. Get it later, Mike thought. Get the hatch open, now—*time's passing!*

Twenty minutes was supposed to be the safe limit to which a man could stay down under this pressure of more than a hundred pounds to the square inch. The pressure pushed from all sides: it had your head in a vise, squeezing it, muddling your thought—it lay heavily against your chest and made you breathe shallowly and fast. . . .

Mike Way knelt clumsily at the hatch. "On deck!" he said. "I'm opening the hatch. I'll need a submarine lamp!"

"Coming down on the descending line," the talker reported.

The hatch shouldn't have given Alexander any trouble, Mike told himself. It yielded with comparative ease. The big chief torpedoman was careful to keep out of its radius as he released the catch; he was guarding against being struck in the event that pressure sealed inside the hull made the cover fly open.

But apparently pressure had been equalized, inside and out. A few good-sized bubbles rumbled out into the sea, and that was all.

And now he was looking down into the blackness of the hatch trunk, down where twenty-two shipmates would be floating in the dark water. The light came down and was added to the equipment he already carried. It wouldn't be an easy task for a man of Mike's size to descend into the hatch carrying all that gear.

He felt dizzy and thick-headed at the same time. He had to keep telling himself why he was down here. Switching on the light, he turned the beam downward. It was equipped with a thousand-watt bulb, but the water showed only a glow, and he could see only a few feet.

"On deck," he reported. "Going into the submarine, now."

"You got ten minutes left, Mike. The Commander says well done on getting Alexander clear, down there. They're taking him aboard, now—they're hustling him into the recompression chamber."

"Damn you!" Mike flared. "I said pipe down! It's no use—he's dead. Understand? Dead! That makes twenty-five!"

He got his legs inside the hatch and began fighting to force his heavy belt through the opening. At the same time, he had to feel with his feet for the rungs of the ladder. Something brushed against his leg and he knew the momentary chill of a thought that he was touching the body of a drowned man. But it was a mattress—somebody had been "caulking off" back here before it happened.

The talker's incoherent voice sounded in his earphones. He swore and throttled down his air.

"The Commander says don't go too far, Mike! You haven't got but eight minutes."

"Hell with that," Mike said thickly.

He fought his way on down.

The lamp gave a little better light in the confines of the torpedo room. Mike swung it forward and saw that the watertight door leading to the engine room had not been shut. This told him how mercifully quickly death had come to the men back here: nobody had had time to close that door against the water, wherever it came from. This compartment was equipped as the torpedo room forward had been— it had the escape hatch, and a smoke bomb and telephone buoy that could be released from the deck above. Nobody had had a chance to send up that distress signal, either.

He turned the light upward, and swung it down again hastily. There were men floating against the overhead, against the maze of pipes and electrical conduits. . . .

"On deck! I'm going forward!"

Slack came freely, but there was always the danger that the lines would foul on something as they paid through the hatch. Mike came to the open door; it was small, and he had to stoop and fight his bulk through it, dragging the underwater torch after him.

He saw more dungaree-clad corpses. One was somehow caught on one of the Diesels that had ceased their throbbing just before the *Starfish* made her fatal dive. Under this deck were the storage batteries that drove the ship under the sea.

The lamp showed him nothing wrong. There wasn't time for a thorough inspection, but he told himself that to come in at such a rate, water would have to pour through a considerable opening. And this compartment looked tight enough.

Another door. It led into the crew's quarters; it was nearly closed. And when Mike Way had struggled through it, his real troubles began.

There were mattresses, mess tables and benches adrift here in a soggy mass. He pushed them out of his way and dropped to his hands and knees to crawl beneath them. They moved sluggishly, then settled in his wake—settled to imperil the free movement of his lines. He could only move by inches, and the clutter of water-logged gear obstructed the rays of his lamp. He saw that several of the men had been trapped here as they slept—men clad only in skivvie shirts and drawers. In the pigboats, there are always men on watch; there are always men sleeping until they are called again.

"On the bottom!" the talker said. "Your time's about up, Chief. The Commander says to allow yourself time to get back out of the submarine."

"Hell with that, too," grunted Mike Way.

He kept crawling. The underwater torch bumped along the deck where the brass-capped toes of his shoes scraped. Ahead of him was the galley door, and beyond that little space that contained the cook's electric range was the door Lieutenant McQuaid had shut while Cardoni screamed and hammered at him. . . .

If Mike Way found anything wrong, this trip, it would have to be in the galley.

He paused, listening, shutting off his air for a few seconds to cut out the roar in his helmet. He thought he had heard a thump on the hull of the submarine. Sounds play queer tricks under water, and nobody knew this better than Mike Way.

The breastplate pressed against his body and shot pain through his sore ribs. He grunted, and turned on the air again as he crawled through the oval door into the galley.

He swung the light around and upward. It showed. him what he had been seeking through all of this dangerous penetration farther into the interior of the *Starfish*.

Overhead was a blower opening off the twenty-four inch main air induction—the huge ventilating pipe which ran aft to feed fresh air, when the submarine was on the surface, to the crew's quarters, the engine room, and the after torpedo room. It was fed by air forced into those vents on the conning tower when the ship was under way. Diving, the big valve at its top was closed—and when this operation had been performed, a red light turned green on that indicator board the pigboat sailors called the "Christmas tree."

Mike Way stood stock still in the small galley, staring at what he saw. The induction was torn and bulged. It was here that the water had come in—a column of water two feet in diameter, with all the pressure of the sea behind it!

He remembered, with an effort, that he had to find out why this had happened. He remembered that day when the diving growler was sounding its loud warning through the ship. All the lights had gone green. . . .

"On deck!" Mike said thickly. His tongue was dry, and clinging to the roof of his mouth. "On deck—turn on the igniter!"

"You'd better come up!" the talker said. "The Commander—"

"Turn on the igniter! I've got to cut away some steel before I can get out of here!"

The talker translated this literally. Off the telephone, Mike heard him say: "He's trapped! He's got to burn his way out. . . ."

Mike pressed the contact points together after adjusting a mixed jet of oxygen, nitrogen and air from the torch supply lines. There was a popping sound, and brilliance burst from the torch nozzle.

He adjusted the valves further and set his lamp down on the electric range. The torch gave more light; it shot a spurt of metal-eating flame more than six feet.

Mike turned it against the main induction. With this torch he could cut inch-thick steel a foot a minute and better.

The flame sheared into the pipe with a roaring sound that drowned all other noises. And then something went wrong.

Mike Way felt the sudden weight of his breastplate. The diving suit hugged his legs. That was where a squeeze always began—down below the knees—

His air was off!

He throttled down the torch, leaving it burning just as little as was possible without losing the jet of flame entirely. "On deck!" he called. "My air—*on deck, there!*"

But the phone was dead, too.

The squeeze crept a little higher on his legs. Mike Way reached to the back of his helmet and closed the exhaust valve to hoard what pressure he had left. At the best, now, he might get out in time to be hoisted to the *Algonquin's* deck more nearly dead than alive. At best, this would mean a horrible case of the bends. . . .

He crawled through the galley door, feeling his way along every inch of his lines in an attempt to discover whether or not some of this clutter of gear had fouled them down here. It was then that he felt an almost imperceptible tug on them—and at the same instant he heard the scrape of a diver's shoes on the rungs of the torpedo room ladder!

His first thought did not concern himself. It was: *Alexander was murdered, too!* Another diver was prowling the blackness of the *Starfish*; the chances were Alexander had been knocked over the side as he knelt to open the hatch. Somebody from the *Westsal!* Kowalski was over there, along with the civilian divers—

Mike Way stopped crawling, stopped feeling his lines as he back trailed. Instead, he got to his feet, holding his breath as long as he dared to conserve his precious air. He thrust himself forward, shouldering aside the floating gear with all the strength of his big, rugged body. An anger as white hot as the jet of flame from that torch drove him on far beyond the point where a weaker man would have stumbled and fallen to die.

In this fashion he came to the door between the torpedo room and the engine room, and saw his man.

The mysterious diver was crouched there, and Mike Way sensed, rather than saw, what he was doing. He had kinked Mike's lines and was holding the kink in them so that virtually all of the life-giving air was shut off; he was sawing at the canvas covering with his knife. The telephone wire had already been cut. At any stroke of the knife, now, the air hose might be severed.

Mike Way lunged forward with the last desperate ounce of his strength and will. The man's helmet came up in the glow of his lamp; the diffused glare of the light was in Mike's eyes, and recognition of the face behind the helmet port was impossible.

But he had seen Mike Way. He came erect in that odd, slow motion style, the lines still kinked in his hand. With the other, he lashed out at the big chief torpedoman.

The knife missed by inches. Mike Way started to reach for his own, but it was a cumbersome job to get the weapon out of that sheath down at his right side. It would be all over before he could free the knife—

Then he remembered the burning underwater torch. He swung the nozzle around and hit the valves. The jet leaped out like a live thing. Its brilliance sizzled against the bulkhead inches from the watertight door; it swung menacingly toward the fragile rubberized canvas suit of the other diver.

One breath of the flame against that suit, and the man who had attempted to kill Mike Way would be dead. . . .

22
CONDITION OF READINESS

Vince Ayres beckoned for Evelyn to accompany him, and went outside the isolation ward. John Thorpe's startling note, expressing willingness to trade a confession for leniency, was still in the doctor's hand.

He passed it to Evelyn. "What do you think of this?"

She read the rounded scrawl twice, first with an exclamation of surprise, and then with a doubtful shake of her head.

"I think he's crazy, after a fashion!" she said. "He wants to attract attention to himself again, Vince. Being locked up below had taken him out of the spotlight. He's grandstanding."

Vince removed his glasses and thoughtfully polished them. "I don't know," he said. "It depends on what he intends to confess."

"Why, the murders—" the girl began, then stopped. She could see what Vince meant.

"Let's take it to the Admiral," he told her. "After all, the old boy is in charge, now. Funny thing about Thorpe, and how we've allowed our hunches and our sympaties to influence us—especially in his case. I only wish the evidence that has pointed to him all along could be directed against somebody I could believe is guilty!"

Evelyn's level brows frowned over an idea. "He picked a strange time to talk, if he really intends to confess to the murders!" she said. "Just when the gun had been found in Barbara West's room. Thorpe didn't put it there, Vince. She knew the gun was there, and it's extremely unlikely that she and Thorpe would be sharing any secret."

"The second-class seaman and the spoiled social butterfly?" Vince smiled. "Hardly!"

He knocked, and the Admiral boomed an invitation for them to enter. His wheelchair was still moored alongside the more stable bed, and the gaunt, shaggy-browed old sea dog had put aside Mahan for a renewed study of the log of the *Starfish*.

He laid this down, and smiled quizzically. Vince went straight to the point.

"Orders placing you in command of the investigation have been posted in the isolation ward, sir," he said. "May I consider myself properly relieved?"

There was something like humor lurking far back in the sea-blue depths of the old man's eyes. Vince and the girl remembered that he had commanded a battleship, in his day, and a whole submarine force.

He said, gruffly, "I relieve you, doctor . . . and now what's on your mind? Oh, by the way—I just received a delayed message from the *Algonquin*. Mike Way has dived again."

Vince and the girl looked at each other in dismay. Vince said, slowly: "Then he's a damned fool! And," he added more softly, "a damned brave man, too."

"What's this likely to do to him?" Admiral Wetherbee asked.

"Nobody could say. Going under pressure again wouldn't hurt him, unless the last dive had strained his heart or something—and in that case the *Algonquin's* medical officer certainly wouldn't permit him to dive. It's the coming up. If there is still some of that nitrogen in his blood, this time he'll have to stay in that recompression tank until he rates another hashmark to be safely decompressed!"

"And I need him here tonight," the Admiral said. "We've got to go into a condition of readiness, as I set forth in the work and drill schedule."

Vince suppressed a smile. The Admiral, he thought, was still playing a game.

"Here's a matter for you to consider," he said, and handed the old man Thorpe's note.

"H'm!" the Admiral said as he read it. "Evelyn, will you please push that button for me? Thank you. Well, I expected the lad to see things my way, after that talk I had with him. This will help, doctor, if it's what I think it is."

A corpsman came to the door and stood respectfully at attention. "Instruct the chief master-at-arms to have John Thorpe, seaman second, lay up to my room right away," the Admiral said.

"Aye, aye, sir!"

"I needed Mike Way," the old man repeated as they waited. "I had expected to hear his report of what he found aboard the *Starfish* in that previous dive, and to go over his report with Lieutenant Brill. Oh, yes, doctor—will you see that Lieutenant Brill is released from his room, when we've finished talking to Thorpe? I see no further reason for his detention."

Evelyn Brill's eyes thanked the Admiral. He chuckled, and added: "When we go into Condition Two, we'll need all hands."

The big chief entered, then with Thorpe. The young survivor of the *Starfish* was trembling, and a pallor was in his thin, nervously drawn features. He stood at attention.

"Stand easy, lad," the Admiral said kindly. "Here—take that chair. Now, we want you to talk freely—tell us everything. Miss Brill, you're prepared to take a record of this?"

"Yes, sir," Evelyn said.

Thorpe's lips quivered. He looked appealingly toward Vince.

"Doctor Ayres, you won't let them—you won't—" he began.

"I can't promise you anything, Thorpe," Vince said. "But I think you should know by now that we're your friends."

"Well," the young sailor began falteringly, "I've thought things over—like you said, sir." He looked at the Admiral. "I've decided I want to stay in the Navy."

Vince Ayres drew a relieved breath. This wasn't going to be a confession of murder, after all.

"I wasn't asleep when I was supposed to be sleepwalking at the hospital and on this ship," Thorpe blurted. "I was putting on, sir. Because—because I wanted out of the Service. I wanted out before I got out of boot camp. But after being shut up down there in the submarine down there in the dark with those fellows aft all dead—I—I thought I couldn't stand it!"

"Go on," Vince said. "Can you tell us where you got the idea of faking somnambulism?"

"I heard about a man who got a medical survey because he walked in his sleep, sir."

"That night at the hospital," the Admiral put in. "You knew the night watchman was going to hit you, didn't you?"

"Not until he had already raised that billiard cue, sir. It was too late to duck, then."

"Why did you carry the billiard cue?" Vince asked.

"Well, this other man I heard about—it was years ago, they told me—was a hospital apprentice. He started parading around at night with a litter on his shoulder and made them think he was dreaming about doing litter drill. I was going to say I dreamed I was carrying a rifle again like we did in boot camp. I—I forgot, after that watchman hit me."

The Admiral rubbed his chin. "And later—aboard the *Consolation*—you were taking advantage of the interest in my logbook when you came in here and picked up the book while pretending to be asleep?"

Thorpe nodded. The old officer seemed pleased at this acknowledgment of interest aroused by his log.

"But you still didn't see or hear anything in the room where Cardoni was killed?" Vince pursued. "Even awake?"

Thorpe shuddered. "No, sir. It was dark. We had turned the lights out. The passageway lights hadn't come on at that time."

"Let's go back to the hospital, and Lieutenant McQuaid's murder," Vince said. "I'll draw a rough diagram of that portion of the buildings. Sick Officers' Quarters ran like this. Odd-numbered quiet rooms and the diet kitchen all had windows opening on the balcony. You were on that balcony, Thorpe."

"Yes, sir," the boy said. "I guess Miss Brill saw me. It was raining and dark. I went over as far as the surgical building on the balcony, but the hall doors were locked over there, and I had to come back. I saw Miss Brill in front of me—she dropped her cape and ran."

"That wasn't Miss Brill," Vince corrected. "It was Barbara West, wearing Miss Brill's cape."

The sailor said, "Oh!" and thought for a minute. "I saw somebody else raising a window, and I had to get away from there because I wanted them to find me down on the grounds, and not on the balcony. So I—"

Vince put the diagram into Thorpe's hands. "Could you remember what window it would have been?" he asked. "And was it being raised from the inside, or out?"

"Inside, sir," Thorpe said. "Let's see. It was here. I know, because the man was standing in the dark. And this room, and the one on the other side were both lighted."

He indicated a window on the diagram. It was Number Three— the quiet room that had not been occupied. It was the room from which a brick had been taken—the brick that battered Lieutenant McQuaid to death.

"I hurried past there," Thorpe was saying, "and went down the balcony to the other wing. There was a door open there, and I got down on the grounds. I had to walk up and down by the fence for a long time before anybody saw me, and then the watchman came and threw his flashlight into my face. The next thing I knew, he grabbed the billiard cue and hit me."

"No wonder," Vince said dryly. "McCarthy was looking for a murderer, by that time. And the person you saw in the dark window was that murderer—on his way out to commit the crime!"

He had no more questions. But the Admiral looked up beneath his shaggy brows. "What were your duties in the *Starfish*, Thorpe?"

"Messcooking, sir. That was one reason I hated it. I—I didn't join the Navy to be a waiter."

"Almost every seaman gets a taste of it," the old man reminded the boy. "In the Navy, we don't always get a billet we like. The Navy's bigger than any of its jobs, any of its men. And as you go along, the better details come your way."

Thorpe hung his head. "I know it now, sir," he said humbly. "If I get off without being kicked out, I'll—I'll messcook, or do whatever they tell me to do, sir."

"You do that," the Admiral answered, "and you're on your way to becoming a man-o'-warsman! I think you can go, now, Thorpe. You aren't under arrest any longer. But, until after tonight, don't make yourself too conspicuous. Understand?"

Thorpe straightened as he stood, squaring his shoulders. He said, "Aye, aye, sir! Thank you, sir!" He was bareheaded, but he saluted. And Admiral Wetherbee, in a wheelchair though he was, returned the salute with the utmost gravity.

"I suppose," he rumbled after the door had closed on Thorpe, "some sort of disciplinary action will have to be taken against that lad. But I hope we can prevent it from being too severe. The Navy is going to make a man out of him!"

"Well," Vince said slowly, "what did we find out? That the murderer went through Number Three quiet room. We already knew he'd been in there to get the brick. The question is, did he enter the room from the hall, or from the balcony?"

"From the hall," Evelyn answered. "Otherwise why should he have had to raise the window from the inside? It would already have been open."

"That's right, young lady," the Admiral approved. "Had it occurred to either of you that perhaps the reason Victor Melhorne didn't answer when Barbara West called to him at his window was because he wasn't in the room at the moment?"

Vince nodded. He'd already considered that possibility. Barbara had said she heard Melhorne's heavy breathing. But she wouldn't be likely to reveal anything that might incriminate the man she was going to marry. And there seemed to be little chance of proving that Melhorne had absented himself from his room. In a hospital hallway, such as that in S.O.Q., several men could have been moving about, coming and going from the washroom, without attracting undue attention. And Miss Wilkins and the corpsmen had been in the diet kitchen.

The Admiral reached for his personal logbook and turned thoughtfully through it. He said, "You will muster your people as usual after supper, doctor. I hope Mike Way will have returned then."

23
SECRET OF THE *STARFISH*

The diver who faced Mike Way's underwater torch at the door of the *Starfish's* engine room had no opportunity to think of the best manner in which to escape having his suit burned in two and dying from the resultant squeeze.

His recoil, slowed by the water, was one of pure reflex action. He twisted, tripped somehow, and dropped to his hands and knees. The jet of flame crackled above him, burning the air out of the chain of tiny bubbles that rose from his exhaust valve. And at the same time, the murderous fury that blazed within the big chief torpedoman burned itself down to a degree that permitted reasoning. He didn't want this man dead on the bottom of the sea—he wanted him alive, for questioning.

Mike throttled down the oxygen-fed flame spurting from the torch nozzle, and held the torch wide from his body and his lines as he thrust his bulk forward. Air was coming back into his suit with full force, and all his vigor returned with it. But in his eagerness to lay hands on the other diver, he forgot one thing.

That was the high storm-step of the oval door that led into the after torpedo room, through which the man was scrambling. Mike barked his canvas-encased shin on the step, hooked the brass cap of his heavy shoe on it, and twisted sidewise. With the steadying weight of his shoe disturbed by its raised position, he doubled over the step and went down on the torpedo room deck.

In the next roaring instant, Mike himself was facing death in a hideous form. The air valve over his left breast caught against the door and was twisted wide open. Air rushed in with mighty force, stretching the suit until he could feel the helmet catching at his chin and threatening to shoot up over his head.

At the same time, the suit was about to spread-eagle him by distending to the point where it flung his arms wide. If that happened, no diver would be strong enough to crook an elbow and reach that air valve; the suit would balloon and blow up—and the squeeze would follow.

The excess air was creating a positive buoyancy that lifted Mike from the deck. His helmet banged with a loud clatter against the overhead. He yelled with this ringing sound in his ears, trying to tell the tender on deck to shut off his air—forgetting that the telephone wire had been severed. And then he managed to hit the spit valve with his chin just as the helmet was about to break his jaw.

Air rushed out in a big bubble. With the last vestige of his strength, Mike Way got his hand over to the valve and closed it.

He sank back to the deck, right side up. And with the roaring gone, he could hear the clumping of diver's shoes on the rungs of the escape hatch ladder.

Whoever the man was, he had escaped.

They'd be anxiously tugging on Mike Way's lines, now, up on the fog-swept deck of the *Algonquin*. Not getting any answer, they'd probably be preparing another diver to come down. Mike moved to the base of the escape hatch and caught hold of his lines to give them a reassuring tug. It was answered immediately.

He grinned, despite himself. That three-striper would be plenty sore because he was overstaying the safe twenty minutes, at this depth.

"Hell!" he muttered in his helmet. "I got a job to do!"

Then he retraced his way forward to the galley, lugging the underwater torch with him. In two or three minutes, he had cut away enough of the main induction to enable him to reach an arm into the big pipe in both directions.

For a little while he groped without result. Then his hand closed on a small object. He brought this out of the steel tube and examined it in the glow of the lamp he had left on the galley range. It was the twisted remains of an ordinary alarm clock.

There was nobody to hear the bitter oaths he shouted into his helmet. In his hand was a clue to the loss of a new, six-million dollar submarine—a clue to the deaths of twenty-two men.

"Twenty-five!" he amended, and cursed again as he retrieved the lamp and the cold torch. He battled his way through the gear adrift in the crew's quarters, he passed the engineman who had been trapped by death at his post, and reached the torpedo room escape hatch. He cleared his lines, and gave four tugs on them as soon as he was out of the hatch trunk,

The diving stage loomed above him at the hundred foot depth, and he cursed the necessity for decompressing here. Topside, now, the man who had been after this same object Mike Way gripped in his hand might be escaping, somehow. . . .

RADIO NINETEENTH NAVAL THIRTEENTH 1825 BT
LIEUT. VINCENT AYRES USS CONSOLATION BT
FINANCIAL POSITION WESTCO IRON WORKS
NONE TOO SECURE DEPENDS ENTIRELY AC-
CEPTANCE OF SUBMARINES NOW BUILDING
LEARNED WEST BORROWED CASH BOND HAS
HAD SOME LABOR TROUBLE AT YARD TROUBLE
APPARENTLY SMOOTHED OUT RECENTLY WHEN
MELHORNE WAS MADE CHIEF ENGINEER IN
ACTIVE CHARGE ATTEMPTING CHECK ON GUNS
SERIAL NUMBER BT
SIMMONS
TOD 1830

It was growing dusk when Vince Ayres signed for the message, read it, and started from his room to deliver it to the Admiral. One of the *Consolation's* hospital corpsmen overtook him at a run in the passageway.

"Dr. Ayres!" the man panted. "Thorpe—he's badly hurt! Maybe dead—"

Vince wheeled. "Thorpe?" he exclaimed. "Good Lord! Where is he?"

"They're taking him into the surgical ward, sir. This way!"

Vince hurried there. Corpsmen were lifting a blue clad figure from a stretcher to a dressing table. Blood streamed down the man's face, and the sturdily-built young stripe-and-a-half doctor was examining a nasty gash on his head.

"Get sutures ready," he told a corpsman. "Let's have some sponges and shears and a razor—the area around the cut will have to be shaved."

"How bad is it?" Vince asked.

The younger doctor looked up. "Only a scalp wound, I'd say, but there may be quite a bit of concussion. The shell weighed quite a bit."

"Shell?"

"Yes—there it is, on that bunk. Somebody dropped it on his head as he came out on the main deck—somebody who was on the deck above!"

Vince looked at the bunk, and saw the missile. It was the babbitt-weighted cartridge case Salty Adams had been converting into a lamp stand. The souvenir Adams had brought out of the *Starfish*.

Vince turned to a corpsman who was merely standing by. "Have the word passed for Adams, first-class torpedoman of the *Starfish* crew!"

"Aye, aye, sir!"

Another corpsman was sponging the blood from the face of the unconscious man. Vince Ayres stepped closer, and then halted in surprise. He bit off the words he was about to say, and turned to the junior grade lieutenant, who was scrubbing up preparatory to suturing the wound.

"How was this man identified, doctor?" Vince asked him in a low voice.

"Why, his white hat was on the deck by him when they found him," the other said. "The stencil says John Thorpe. Isn't he—"

"No. He's not Thorpe. My guess is that he's another of the men from the *Starfish*, and was just wearing Thorpe's white hat. Those people had to leave practically all of their clothing in the submarine, and were given dry clothes when they came aboard."

The other doctor said, "That's right. But why—"

"It was an attempt to murder John Thorpe within a couple of hours after he'd been released from the storeroom where he was locked up," Vince said grimly. "Whoever did it read that stencil on the hat from the deck above, seized the first weapon he could find, and dropped it. It's a wonder this man's alive."

The junior grade officer nodded. "Fortunately, it struck a glancing blow."

Salty Adams was coming into the ward, his sea going nonchalance shattered for once. Vince said, "Please say nothing about the mistaken identity. I think it might help us if word is allowed to get around that Thorpe is dying from a cranial injury."

"I understand, Dr. Ayres," said the other.

Vince turned to meet Adams. "Get your lamp and come with me," he told the first-class torpedoman.

They went to Admiral Wetherbee's room. Salty Adams was as mystified as anybody over the attack.

"I was in the radio shack, asking one of the radio gadgets to find out how Mike Way is doing," he said. "I didn't even know the lamp was gone from my room!"

"Where is your room?" Vince asked.

It was on the promenade deck, well aft. The door had been open—Adams shared the room with another man from the *Starfish*. "Anybody could have walked in and picked up the lamp," he said.

Admiral Wetherbee sent at once for the chief master-at-arms, then turned a quizzical look on Vince. He said, "Well, who was it this time? They're all aboard—Kowalski, Melhorne and Bedell returned from the *Westsal* more than an hour ago. So we can't eliminate anyone by reason of absence. Any chance of getting fingerprints off that three-inch cartridge case? Brass records prints easily, as any man who's ever polished brightwork in the Navy knows."

Vince shook his head. "When Thorpe was found, they thought it was an accident, sir. Probably a half dozen men handled that lamp before we brought it back here. And I have an idea the person we are dealing with is far too clever not to think of taking precautions against leaving fingerprints. It would have been a simple matter for him to handle that lamp stand with a handkerchief, or something else."

The big chief entered. Admiral Wetherbee said, "Find Thorpe and lock him up again. Don't let anybody see you do this, and don't mention it to anyone. Thorpe is supposed to have been very badly hurt—in fact, he's about to die. That comes straight from the scuttle-butt, chief, and you can spread it."

"Aye, aye, sir!" the master-at-arms said. "Thorpe's already below, sir. I was having him clean up that storeroom where he stayed."

"Very good," the Admiral said. "Just keep him there."

They dismissed Salty Adams. Vince sank into a chair. "Well," he mused, "the murderer has scored two misses in a row. Maybe he'll strike out. He appears to be slipping, but, so far as I can see, he's still slipping through our fingers. Here is a bit of information I just received from Intelligence, sir. It doesn't clarify the situation very much."

The Admiral scarcely glanced at the yellow communications sheet. "Yes, I received the same intelligence—along with other in-formation which may and may not be pertinent. But I think you are being overly pessimistic when you say our man is slipping through our fingers, doctor. . . . By the way, have you been told that the *Con-solation* has received orders to return to port?"

Vince looked up in surprise. "No, I haven't. When?"

"Orders came from the Commandant a little while ago. The ship isn't needed here now that all the *Starfish* survivors are aboard, and raising of the submarine may be left to the civilian salvage crew. We are to get under way as soon as Mike Way has been returned aboard. Now—let's take a look at this work and drill schedule of mine. '2030 Go into Condition of Readiness No. 2. All hands battle stations. Dark-en ship. 2040—or when contact is made—Trap murderer.'"

"Just how literally is that schedule to be interpreted?" Vince interrupted with a shade of annoyance. "Have you actually arranged for the ship to be darkened at half past eight—we may be under way by that time—or is this a smoke screen?"

The Admiral smiled. "I am referring to the only portion of this ship over which I exercise any control at all," he said with gentle dignity. "This room. Now, let's discuss the strategy and tactics to be employed. . . ."

Mike Way was back in the iron doctor aboard the *Algonquin*, fully conscious, this time, and suffering from no physical pain. Mentally, however, he died an agonizing death with each crawling minute.

"Come on—shake it up—shake it up!" he begged the pharmacist's mate who had entered the chamber with him. "I've got to get out of here!"

"Keep your shirt on, Chief," the corpsman returned mildly. "The *Consolation* won't sail without you. You'll be back aboard that bed-pan barge in about two hours. Isn't that fast enough?"

"Hell, no!" Mike growled. He swung one of the heavy diver's socks he had worn. It was still wet from the water that had leaked into his suit through the side of his exhaust valve. And now it was stuffed with the clock he had removed from the main induction of the *Starfish*.

The pharmacist's mate grinned. "You're not in a hurry," he kidded. "Not with three hashmarks on your sleeve. I guess you've got plenty of time to do in this outfit—if I had that much time to do, I'd go over the hill!"

"Sure!" the big chief torpedoman flared. "I'm a thirty-year man. And where do I spend my time? In the damn tanks!"

The needle on the pressure dial swung slowly to the left each time air was valved out of the chamber. The heat of compression decreased with the needle's crawl, and the nitrogen bubbles in Mike Way's blood were working off in the same proportion. He inhaled from an oxygen mask to speed the action of his respiratory and circulatory systems—and he very nearly got on an oxygen jag.

But it was a full two hours before the door was opened and he stepped out into fresh, foggy air. Darkness had crept in over the sea. He waited for what seemed a long time before the motor sailer from the *Consolation* chugged alongside. It had made another trip earlier, and there was a flag-draped casket in the *Consolation*. Alexander's. *Twenty-five,* Mike Way told himself.

He had asked no questions aboard the *Algonquin*, nor had he told those in the salvage tug anything of that desperate battle forty fathoms down. It wasn't unusual for a telephone line to be severed against some sharp surface while a diver was working in a submarine.

But now there was one more jigsaw fragment fitted into place, and the pattern of remembered horror had begun to take fantastic shape. And there was that blue sock, with the lump that suggested Christmas eve—the lump itself filled a vacant space in the puzzle of mystery and murder.

Mike Way held the sock carefully as he climbed the accommodation ladder to the *Consolation's* deck. "Reporting aboard after diving duty, sir!" he announced to the officer of the deck, and then faced aft to salute the quarterdeck.

A bosun's pipe shrilled, and a detail of seamen immediately set to work shipping the accommodation ladder and securing it for sea.

24
THE ADMIRAL DARKENS SHIP

Vince Ayres mustered his party in the isolation ward just after sup-per, calling the roll while Evelyn checked off the absentees. Every-body answered to his name except John Thorpe and Mike Way. Lieu-tenant Everett Brill, freshly shaven and wearing service dress blues some officer in the *Consolation* had lent him, was back. He still wore a worried look, Vince noticed, and two days of confinement seemed to have added remarkably to the paleness of his once red face.

Vince looked up after the roll had been called. "We all know what happened to young Thorpe," he said quietly. "I can tell you nothing, except that he is still alive."

Victor Melhorne's pale eyes plainly said, "I told you so!" He had criticized Vince Ayres, the doctor remembered, for failure to keep Thorpe locked up. Foster Bedell pursed his lips and scrubbed his jaw with his palm.

"Mike Way dived again today, despite the fact that he suffered a bad attack of bends last night," Vince went on. "I don't expect that he will be able to attend this hearing—in fact, he may have to be left aboard the *Algonquin*. As you also know, we are scheduled to get un-der way in a few minutes."

Martin West shifted his big bulk uncomfortably. He said, "What happens when we reach port? Will Melhorne and Bedell and I be re-leased from—from this damned ship?"

Vince spread his hands and noted the expressions of the three civilians. West was angry and importantly annoyed; Bedell's dark face was intense. Melhorne wore his customary cold, efficient-look-ing engineer's expression.

181

"That will be a matter for the district authorities to decide," Vince informed them. He sighed, and added: "I'm afraid all of us are in for a siege of intensified questioning and investigation. You may as well understand the Navy's determination to get to the bottom of this affair. Doubtless Admiral Wetherbee will be relieved by an active duty officer in the district. He'll be new on the job, with only the Admiral's log and the transcript Miss Brill has kept to work from. Naturally, he'll have questions of his own to ask."

"That's all very well," Melhorne said. "But we have a ship to raise."

Foster Bedell shrugged. "Perhaps," he said quietly, "it would be possible for each of us to make a deposition covering all that we know—or, I should say—all we don't know, after which we might be permitted to get back to work. I think Mr. West might be able to arrange that."

Martin West swelled slightly at this tribute to his importance. His daughter patted his hand and smiled at him. Vince said, "I hope you are able to proceed with the salvage operations without delay. Well, let's get on with this business. Mr. Melhorne—we'll begin with you, please!"

The anchor chain was rumbling up as Melhorne went silently into the glass-enclosed nurse's office. Evelyn and Vince followed; the doctor motioned for Melhorne to take a chair. Looking outside, he could see the anxiety in Barbara West's dark eyes.

Melhorne said, with chill sarcasm, "I understood there would be no more need of this! Didn't Admiral Wetherbee say he knows who the murderer is?"

Vince faced him quietly. "I'll read you the latest radio report received by the Admiral from Naval Intelligence ashore, Mr. Melhorne."

RADIO NINETEENTH NAVAL THIRTEENTH 1840 BT
REAR ADMIRAL J. K. WETHERBEE USS CONSOLA-
TION BT
RECORD OF FIREARMS SALES SHOWS THIRTY
TWO CALIBER AUTOMATIC THAT MAKE AND SE-
RIAL NUMBER PURCHASED LAST MONTH BY VIC-
TOR MELHORNE BT
SIMMONS
TOD 1847

Melhorne stiffened. "You mean," he demanded, "that it was my gun used in the attempt to kill Mike Way?"

"Exactly," Vince said.

"Then it was stolen from my room," the engineer said. "I hadn't missed it. Where is the gun, now?"

Vince took it from his coat pocket and handed it over to the other man. Barbara West could see this move through the glass. She put a nervous hand to her lips. She was still afraid, Vince thought, that Victor Melhorne was the murderer.

The shipyard engineer examined the weapon in silence. There was a throb of engines under the deck; the *Consolation* trembled, and listed slightly as she turned under the thrust of her screws.

Melhorne said, "Yes, it's mine. I bought it last month, because we were having a little trouble at the Westco yard—a racketeer, a so-called labor leader, was attempting to throw a wrench into our production schedule. And, in times like these, you can't take too many precautions against spies and saboteurs—not when you're working on Government contracts."

"We were interrupted when I questioned you before," Vince said. "You appeared rather certain that young Thorpe was guilty. I think you'll agree subsequent events have tended to disprove that."

"Well?" Melhorne parried.

"You didn't mention saboteurs, then. You will agree that the pattern of things makes it appear that the murders are definitely linked to the sinking of the *Starfish*. Would you say sabotage could have been responsible for that sinking?"

"Certainly, it *could* have been!" Melhorne snapped. "But I was aboard, and I saw no evidence of it. It's my belief that the human element was responsible."

Vince smiled faintly. Melhorne was echoing the words of Martin West, his employer, in intimating that Everett Brill had given the order for the full crash dive before his ship was rigged for diving.

He said, "Well, it isn't the duty of this inquiry, of course, to branch into a technical investigation as to the causes of that disaster. We are only interested, officially, in any connection between the sinking and the murders. I think that will be all, just now, Mr. Melhorne."

He looked at his watch. It was five after eight. The ship was under way, and that meant Mike Way had returned aboard—unless, indeed, he had been forced to stay in the recompression chamber aboard the *Algonquin*.

Melhorne made no move to go. He squirmed under the first real uneasiness he had ever displayed, and he asked the question Vince had known he would ask.

"Where was the gun found, doctor?"

Vince watched him carefully. "In Miss West's room."

Melhorne sprang to his feet. "Then it was planted there!" he exclaimed. "The murderer is attempting to evade detection by switching the blame to her. She's entirely innocent!"

"I'm inclined to believe you're right, and I certainly hope so," Vince said gently. "But the fact remains that she knew the gun was there, and the fact also remains that you've been very much afraid that she isn't entirely innocent! Just as she has feared that you aren't."

"That's a lie!" Melhorne blazed. "You're only—"

"Just a minute!" Vince said. "Nobody is accusing either of you. But I can suggest a course of action you should take immediately. Sit down with Miss West and have a heart-to-heart talk. Tell each other, freely, all that you know, and remove this fear—which amounts to suspicion—from each other's mind."

A corpsman knocked on the door, and Evelyn admitted him. He handed Vince a sheet torn from the Admiral's logbook.

Victor Melhorne drew a long breath. "Thank you, Dr. Ayres," he said sincerely. "I believe that would be a wise thing to do!"

He went out into the ward. Evelyn said, "That was very kind of you, Dr. Beatrice Fairfax. But will it help the investigation any for them to compare stories and agree on an airtight account?"

Vince grinned at her. "They'd have done that, anyway, sooner or later," he said. "And if they're in love, why let them suffer?" He removed his glasses, polishing them and looking almost boyish without them as he continued to smile at the girl. "I wouldn't want you to feel that way about me, Evelyn," he added.

She looked down, and the clear color came into her cheeks. "You mean you wouldn't want me to be in love with you?" she asked softly.

Vince Ayres knew in that moment that he had won one case, at least—one far more important than the solution of a murder mystery.

He said, "You darling! I'll discuss that with you a little later. Come on into the ward."

Outside he cleared his throat and announced that he had just received an order from Admiral Wetherbee. It was written in the old man's neat, precise hand, and it conformed to the pattern prescribed for official correspondence. Vince read it aloud:

FROM: Rear Admiral J. K. Wetherbee USN (Retd.)

To: Lieut. Vincent Ayres, (MC) USN.

SUBJECT: Murder inquiry, cessation of.

1. Pursuant to orders of this date from the Commandant, Nineteenth Naval District and Operating Base, you will cease present activities bearing on the investigation into the murder of Lieut. Frederick McQuaid, USN, and subsequent crimes.

2. All transcript of testimony and other data obtained will be prepared in typewritten form for the scrutiny, along with Admiral Wetherbee's personal log, of a board of inquiry to be convened in the *Consolation* as soon after her arrival in port as circumstances will permit.

J. K. WETHERBEE

Rear Admiral, USN (Retd.)

There was a momentary silence in the ward when Vince had finished reading. Then Melhorne said, disgustedly: "The Admiral's log will be of great help, I'm sure!"

"More than you—or even I—know," Vince answered. "You must remember that he sleeps very little. He was awake that night when McQuaid was killed. We have seen only the portions of the logbook which he wanted us to see."

Barbara West stood with a little toss of her head. "Does this mean we are free to go, now?" she asked sarcastically.

"You may," Vince nodded. "As my last official act in connection with this somewhat unpleasant duty of which I have just been relieved, I would like to thank all of you for your co-operation. And," he added with grim significance, "to wish each of you the best of luck!"

Melhorne took Barbara West's arm and hurried her out of the ward with a polite nod to Vince. The others filed past him to shake his hand as if he were, indeed, relinquishing a Navy command. Martin West said, "I'm sorry if we haven't appeared to be doing all we could to help, doctor. There's been so much on my mind . . ."

Foster Bedell said, "You actually made it a pleasure to be questioned, Dr. Ayres. I hope the shore board is as kind." And Everett Brill gripped his hand warmly.

"They handed you a tough detail," he declared. "You did the best you could with the tools you had."

That was a Navy maxim. Hearing it, Vince felt better. But he alone of the people in the ward knew that the night's work was not yet completed—not if the Admiral's plans could be counted on to work out properly.

The Admiral looked at his watch. Twenty-nine past eight—2029 by the Navy's twenty-four hour clock. He maneuvered his wheel chair a couple of feet to starboard, which was not an easy performance with the roll of the ship, and placed his copy of Mahan on his bedside locker. Then, as if by an afterthought, he shuffled the books there so that his log was on top.

Only the reading lamp was burning at the head of his bed. Admiral Wetherbee muttered to himself, "Darken ship!" and switched out his light.

As if this were a signal, the partly open door widened to admit the shadowy figure of a big man who carried a bulky burden.

He asked in a low tone, "All set, sir?"

"Carry out your mission," the Admiral chuckled. He was enjoying every moment of this, just as he had enjoyed fighting in two wars and playing at fighting a score of others in the Navy's annual Fleet Problems. Once more he was employing strategy against the enemy—an enemy as invisible as if his masts were over the far horizon.

The big man moved to the bed and turned down the covers. He arranged the bulky object he had carried beneath them.

"You're sure you don't want me to stand by in here, sir?" he whispered.

"Take your battle station!" the Admiral answered, and the other went out.

One bell sounded faintly from the bridge of the *Consolation*. The Admiral countermarched his wheel chair forward, turned it smartly in the darkness, and came to a full stop. He was near the forward bulkhead some twelve feet from his bed, and now he settled down to his vigil.

A single light had been left burning in the passageway. The Admiral's partly opened door swung gently with the ship's rolling, admitting a faint glow that was bluish and unreal into that portion of the room occupied by the bed. The Admiral sat fully erect, his plaster-encased leg thrust straight out before him on the wheel chair footrest.

When a man is seventy, he has learned patience; when he is a Navy man, he has learned it long before. Waiting here in the darkness, the Admiral could listen to the rhythmical wash of the sea along the side and hear the thump of the screws beneath; he could even see a star, now and then, swinging across one of the portholes like the trucklights on a tall ship. This was not greatly different from other watches he had stood in the blackness of nights long past, straining his eyes from the bridge of his ship, responsibility lying heavily on his gaunt shoulders.

The responsibility was there now, he told himself, and he remembered with a pang of regret that tomorrow the *Consolation* would be back in harbor, moored prosaically alongside a dock. Well, it was something to have gone to sea again, even if only for a little while. . . .

He wished he had thought to have somebody raid the officers' galley or one of the diet kitchens for a cold turkey leg and a bottle of milk.

The minutes were long. After an endless procession of them, he heard two bells on the bridge. Nine o'clock—2100—and he was already behind schedule. And the silvery-sweet, sad music of taps was sounding through the ship; the last note lingered and was blended and lost in the song of the sea's running along the hull plates. Other lights were going out, now; there was silence between the decks.

It was only a little time, then, until the Admiral's door opened a trifle wider—opened so softly no one could have heard. There had been no sound in the passageway; there was none now in the room. Shadows do not make sound, and it was a shadow moving here in the gloom.

The shadow moved silently near the bed, within easy reach of the locker where Mahan and the Admiral's logbook lay. The old man who watched saw the shadow raise an arm. The dim light shone faintly on the blade of a large knife.

25
"CEASE PRESENT EXERCISES!"

Mahan had said: "The enemy must not be fended off, but smitten down. . . ." And Admiral Wetherbee went suddenly into action under his precept.

The prowler whirled, still crouching, still holding the knife out from his body, and the Admiral heard his muttered exclamation. He had sensed that a trap was set here: that that was no man lying in the Admiral's bed, but merely a Navy hammock, rolled and lashed for stowing.

But the strange, wheeled attack came swiftly out of the darkness and there was no time to prepare to meet it. The Admiral sent the chair into motion with a powerful thrust of his arms, and the roll of the ship helped to give him momentum.

He let out a yell that would have been loud in the teeth of a Cape Race blizzard. The jar sent a shock running through his out-thrust leg, and the wheel chair careened dizzily against the bed.

The prowler buckled with a grunt of pain, and grabbed at the bed-side locker in a futile effort to preserve his balance. That footrest had rammed him just above the knees; he fell rolling on the sloping deck, and the locker came down with a shower of books and hospital gear.

The long knife flew from the man's hand. Admiral Wetherbee hurled his gaunt body from the wheel chair, forgetting to favor the plaster-weighted leg in his eagerness to attack.

Ensuing seconds were violent and loud and confused. The Admiral grappled with the enemy he had smitten down, but his momentum carried him on; he rolled over the man's wiry, desperately struggling form, and brought up against the bulkhead near the door. In the next instant the man leaped to his feet and darted into the passageway.

"All hands!" bellowed the Admiral. "Look lively, out there!"

He rolled through the door, hampered by the plaster cast and the nautical discovery that it wouldn't clear the doorway fore and aft, but had to be turned athwartships. Somebody leaped over his leg and landed running. The dimly lighted passageway was loud with shouts and action.

Vince Ayres ran past, headed aft. Vince shouted: "Look out, Mike—*he's got a gun!*"

The Admiral came right-side-up outside his door. Aft he saw the prowler fleeing up the ladder leading to the promenade deck, with the hand chains giving off a frantic rattle. The old sea dog smiled grimly, for he had arranged to have that hatch cover temporarily secured, and there was no opening at the top of the ladder.

The man in the peacoat was trapped. Big Mike Way lunged up the ladder, clutching at his ankles. The man kicked desperately at Mike's face. The gun was in his hand.

Mike Way ignored the gun. Vince Ayres charged to the chief torpedoman's aid, but there was no more room on the ladder. Mike Way leaped up it again with a savage fury.

The gun laid a loud, reverberating noise into the passageway, and Admiral Wetherbee didn't want to look. He heard the heavy roll and thump down the ladder. . . .

And then he heard Mike Way's panting voice. The big chief torpedoman swore.

"He shot himself! It's—it's Foster Bedell!"

It was nearly an hour before the excitement had died away and Admiral Wetherbee was propelled forward to the isolation ward where Captain McKee had ordered the *Starfish* survivors and the party from the hospital to assemble. The Captain himself was on hand; he rose respectfully as the old sea dog was wheeled in, and everybody else came to attention. It was almost like going aboard a ship to inspect it, or to pay an official call; the Admiral needed only sideboys and the shrill of a bosun's pipe to complete the illusion.

He said, gruffly, "Carry on!" and they sat down with the Admiral facing them.

Captain McKee said, "Well, sir—we're all waiting to hear what happened, and how you did it."

"I?" the Admiral repeated. "I didn't stir. The credit belongs to Dr. Ayres, and to Miss Brill, and—above all—to Chief Mike Way! But,"—and he smiled—"when a sailor gets old, he loves to spin yarns. So I'll tell you how. Mike, give me that sock."

The big chief brought it forward. Admiral Wetherbee reached inside and drew out the shattered and twisted remains of the clock, its dial still intact but faded by sea water.

"This," he said, "is enough to explain what happened in the *Starfish*. This is what is left of a time bomb which Foster Bedell placed in the main induction that ventilated the after-compartments—he planted it at a point where it would unseat the valve at the instant of explosion, without doing a great amount of damage to the induction itself."

Lieutenant Brill uttered an exclamation, and James, the executive officer, snapped bolt upright. "But, Admiral Wetherbee," the dapper little officer said, "Bedell couldn't have had a chance to place any bomb there that day! And besides, would he have done it when he knew he'd be aboard, himself?"

"This chronometer," the Admiral explained, "was of a fairly reliable and accurate make. It would run eight days. Sometime within eight days before the disaster, Bedell had the opportunity to plant the bomb."

He held up the log of the *Starfish*. "I began to suspect a time bomb the first time I examined Captain Brill's log. This log shows that test maneuvers had been executed on the minute according to a schedule laid down a week or two in advance! Very commendable promptness, Brill—the Navy must move on time. Well, Foster Bedell also noticed this strict adherence to schedule. He expected the supreme test of the *Starfish's* trials—the full crash dive—would take place at 1530 on 9 January. He set his chronometer accordingly. It was no trick for a man with Bedell's technical skill to manufacture a bomb."

Martin West's heavy face was gray as he shook his head. "I don't believe it!" he burst out harshly. "I can't believe it! *Why?* Why would he have done it?"

"We will come to that presently," the Admiral said. "Now, Lieutenant James, you ask whether a man would seek to destroy a ship when he was aboard. The answer is that Bedell didn't think he'd be aboard, and he didn't expect, when he planted his bomb, that anybody would die. He knew there'd be noise enough to muffle the slight explosion required to unseat the valve. The dive would have just been started—at 1530, remember—and chances were the sub could have surfaced, with only an amount of water shipped aft and nobody hurt. At the time, the incident would have been laid to a structural weakness—and before the main induction was removed for a thorough examination, Bedell would have fished out his bomb."

Victor Melhorne had been sitting with shoulders hunched and his bleak eyes staring at the bulkhead. Barbara West was close at his side, holding his hand in both of hers. Melhorne shook himself now, like a man surprised out of a trance.

"Why, it could be that way!" he said in his metallic voice. "You remember, Mr. West—Bedell was to have been at the yards after the first week of the *Starfish's* trials. The day before the full crash dive, we decided it would be better to have two observers aboard. Bedell was to be stationed forward, checking the trim of the ship. I remember now, that he spent a great deal of time aft up to a minute or two before the dive was made."

"I saw him in the galley, sir," John Thorpe remembered. "He came in there several times."

Admiral Wetherbee nodded. "Yes, he was looking for a chance he didn't get—a chance to remove the bomb. He could have confessed, then, what he had done. But he didn't, because that would have ruined him. He still was reasonably certain there would be no loss of life. Bedell didn't make a mistake, but his chronometer did! Captain Brill held to his schedule, and the ship dived at 1530. Bedell's chronometer had lost almost a minute, by then. Because of that, the submarine was just so much farther under the surface. Because of that—" and the old sea dog paused dramatically "—all those men died. Then Bedell *couldn't* confess."

Vince Ayres said, "I fail to see why an explosion wouldn't have been heard."

"Well," Everett Brill said slowly, "if it had been a big one, of course it would have been heard. But we had shifted control to below, so nobody was in the conning tower. The warning growler was going. The sea was rough and slamming against the conning tower when the eyeports went awash. I suppose most of the sound traveled aft, through the induction."

"Perhaps the men aft *did* hear it," said Admiral Wetherbee. "Who's left to tell about any sound? Only Thorpe. A man can forget a little thing such as a noise, under the strain of what followed. But McQuaid—the one man who could have told us what happened—did remember one thing. The smell."

Brill looked up quickly. "You mean it wasn't—" he began.

"It wasn't any smell of liquor McQuaid was trying to tell about, subconsciously. It was the smell of powder, Captain—the fumes of whatever explosive Bedell used. The smell was forced down the induction by the inrushing water."

Martin West buried his gray face in his stubby hands, then pushed his hands upward across his forehead as if trying to erase from his memory all that had happened. Failing, he said wearily:

"But why, Admiral? Why? Foster Bedell helped build that ship. He was a good engineer—one of the best. He'd been with me more than five years!"

"Exactly," the Admiral said. "Those were all reasons he thought he should have been retained as chief engineer. Mr. Melhorne was promoted to that post over Bedell, and Bedell nursed a grudge. I suspect he knew of Miss West's secret betrothal to Melhorne, too. Anyway, the day after Melhorne's promotion, Bedell went to see your chief competitor about a job."

"Pacific Maritime?" West asked in a surprised tone.

"Yes. His chance of getting a position with them as their chief engineer depended on Pacific Maritime's chances of grabbing off at least a part of the government contracts. So he planned to make the *Starfish* design appear faulty. He—"

"Just a minute, please!" Melhorne's brittle voice broke in. "How did you learn so much of Bedell's movements, sir?"

"Captain Brill's log revealed Bedell was aboard the first week of the trials, was detached, and returned later. As for the other information—I've had Intelligence checking the records of everybody, ashore."

"Go on, please," Captain McKee requested. "How would Bedell have made the sinking appear an accident?"

"He dived yesterday—that is, it's yesterday now—to remove the evidence of that bomb. He went down from the *Westsal*. I checked on that too. You didn't dive, Kowalski?"

"No, sir," answered the curly-headed sailor.

"That was a diver's knife Bedell dropped in my room, after he'd put on a bluejacket's uniform. Mr. Melhorne knew that Bedell dived, but he doesn't know what happened. Tell them, chief."

Mike Way recounted the attempt to kill him by severing his air line, and how Bedell must have killed Alexander a little earlier.

"It was foggy, sir," the big chief said. "The *Westsal* didn't report to the *Algonquin* that she had a diver down. She should have, because the lines might have become tangled."

"Bedell reported that the *Algonquin had* been notified," Melhorne declared. "We weren't right over the submarine. He had to walk a way after reaching the bottom. He phoned up that he was inspecting the hull from the outside."

"And he saw the slack in Alec's lines, hanging over the side!" Mike Way exclaimed. "He pulled Alec down, and jammed the lines under the stern planes. It was slow work climbing aboard, and by that time I was inside."

"Bedell *had* to be first in the flooded compartments," Admiral Wetherbee pointed out. "He knew Mike Way had found something suspicious on that first dive, but he didn't know what. It was a portion of this chronometer's stout steel spring blown out through the unseated valve and sticking through a vent. Bedell thought if he could remove everything in the way of bomb fragments, water pressure might be blamed for the bulge and the ripping of the induction."

"How about the others?" asked Vince Ayres. "The murders?"

"Bedell knew McQuaid had smelled the powder. He went through that vacant quiet room, got the brick, and picked up Evelyn's cape on the balcony. He watched from outside until the corpsman left McQuaid's room to get that ice cap, and he timed his blows to the corpsman's chopping of the ice.

"But if McQuaid had smelled the powder, perhaps Cardoni had, too, and Cardoni might remember when the shock had worn off. So he killed Cardoni. He didn't try to kill Thorpe just then, because Thorpe himself was under suspicion, and it was worth Bedell's while to let him live.

"Then Mike Way was about to reveal something he'd found on the submarine, and Bedell knew it. He had a gun of his own, but it was smart to use another man's gun, and he knew Melhorne had one in his room. He missed Mike Way, nearly got caught, and had to get rid of the gun. If it had been his own, he certainly would have thrown it over the side. But it was to his advantage to cast suspicion somewhere else."

The Admiral paused, smiling at Barbara West. "I think," he said kindly, "that you could tell us what he did with that automatic, Miss West."

The girl flushed uncomfortably. "Yes, I can. He must have opened Victor's door, saw nobody was in, and tossed the gun on the bunk. I went there looking for Victor, and saw it. I was afraid—you can understand that."

"Perfectly," the Admiral smiled.

"Well, I hid the gun in my room. I'm sorry, now, that I denied it later. I was—"

"You were in love, young lady," the Admiral said. "That just about finishes the story. Except that Bedell began to see that Thorpe was clearing himself in spite of all the circumstantial evidence, and he came back from the *Westsal* just in time to try killing Thorpe by dropping that cartridge case on his head. It happened to be another man who was wearing Thorpe's white hat, and I'm happy to inform you the man isn't seriously hurt."

"Now," he went on half-humorously, "I have some confessions of my own to make. In the first place, my logbook never did contain anything of real importance. Dr. Ayres and Miss Brill helped create the illusion that it held the key to the mystery, however, and I helped build up that bit of camouflage by arranging for a message from shore, ordering me to take charge. That was only more strategy, doctor, and I assure you the Commandant understood it as such."

Vince smiled back. "It doesn't matter whether he did or not, sir. You're being too modest. You built the trap, set it, and sprung it when Bedell attempted to kill you and get that logbook. Finally, you charged Bedell in a wheel chair."

"Mechanized forces afloat," murmured the Admiral. He looked at his watch. "It's late, and I suggest that we get to bed. Most people sleep this time of morning."

But there were dozens who wanted to shake hands with him. Barbara West gave him a hug that left lipstick on his gaunt, leathery cheek. And tall, military-looking Captain McKee made a remark that sent happiness tingling through the Admiral's veins.

"Too damn bad," the Captain declared, "that the Government sees fit to retire some men in the prime of their lives!"

Later, the Admiral propelled his wheel chair out to the open deck where he could feel wind on his face and watch the stars swinging overhead. The fog was gone. There was no longer a ring around the moon to denote stormy weather ahead. The music of wind and wave was sweeter than anything the Admiral had ever heard—that is, until he heard a girl's low, happy laugh at the rail.

It was Evelyn Brill. Vince Ayres stood very near to her. Without the slightest feeling of guilt at eavesdropping, the Admiral saw Vince put his arms around her and lift her chin for a long kiss.

He chuckled slyly to himself, then, and propelled the wheel chair back to his room. There was a note lying on his logbook. He read it, smiled happily, and made an entry in his log:

U. S. S. CONSOLATION 14 January.
At Sea, enroute Nineteenth Naval District.
    0105 Secured from General Quarters.
    0130 Admiral J. K. WETHERBEE, U. S. N. (Retd.) hauled down his flag, relinquishing temporary command of murder investigation.
    0138 Lieut. Vincent AYRES (MC) U. S. N. finally cleared decks for action. When last sighted, he was engaged at very close quarters and seemed to have the situation well in hand. . . .

0143 Received official confirmation of victory won by Lieut. AYRES, in form of wedding invitation, ceremony to take place 22 January (or as soon thereafter as resignation of BRILL, Evelyn, from N. N. C. can be effected.)

NOTE: I hope all their sons are midshipmen.

COACHWHIP PUBLICATIONS

CoachwhipBooks.com

THE CAT
SCREAMS

A HUGH RENNERT MYSTERY

Todd Downing

COACHWHIP PUBLICATIONS
CoachwhipBooks.com

COACHWHIP PUBLICATIONS
COACHWHIPBOOKS.COM

CRIME IN
CORN-WEATHER

MARY MEIGS ATWATER

COACHWHIP PUBLICATIONS
COACHWHIPBOOKS.COM

MURDER
IN TEXAS

Ada E. Lingo

"The story of a big-time murder in
a small town, with the atmosphere
of a hard-boiled newspaper office,
a background of 'hot oil' and
sudden gushers, and the intensity
of a Texas heat wave."

COACHWHIP PUBLICATIONS
CoachwhipBooks.com

AN AMOS LEE MAPPIN MYSTERY

HULBERT FOOTNER

UNNEUTRAL
MURDER

COACHWHIP PUBLICATIONS
COACHWHIPBOOKS.COM

THE INVISIBLE
BULLET

& OTHER STRANGE CASES OF
MAGNUM, SCIENTIFIC CONSULTANT

MAX RITTENBERG

www.ingramcontent.com/pod-product-compliance
Lightning Source LLC
Chambersburg PA
CBHW020647260626

47157CB00008B/2939